LEVON'S HOME

A VIGILANTE JUSTICE THRILLER
BOOK 8

CHUCK DIXON

ROUGH
EDGES
PRESS

Rough Edges Press
An Imprint of Wolfpack Publishing
701 S. Howard Ave. 106-324 Tampa, Florida 33609

roughedgespress.com

Paperback ISBN 978-1-68549-043-0
eBook ISBN 978-1-68549-033-1

LEVON'S HOME

1

It was stifling in the cellar under the house, airless and musty. Working the shovel under the low ceiling had Dean sweating through his T-shirt inside a minute. His close-cropped hair was sopping on his scalp, stinging rivulets cresting over his brows.

"Why do I got to do this?" he asked the older boy seated on the wooden steps, drinking pop from a can.

"'Cause you the right height for the job," Sonny said. He held out the can for Dean to take a long slurp. Sonny swiped an errant strand of his long ginger hair from his eyes.

Dean saw the reasoning. Even for his ten years, he was shorter than most boys. At fourteen, Sonny was already too tall to stand up straight under the wooden beams above.

"'S hard workin' bent over like this," Dean said.

"Then dig faster so you can stand in the hole."

"Ground's hard."

"If ditch diggin' were easy, ever'body'd want to d'it."

"This ain't a ditch."

"Same as." Sonny took a long pull on the pop before crushing the can and tossing it to a dark corner.

Dean sat at the lip of the uneven depression he'd made in the earth floor. He pulled up the hem of his sodden shirt to wipe sweat from his face. Another foot or two to go before the bundle at the foot of the stairs would fit in the hole. It was a sad little package, wrapped tight in contractor bags and duct tape. Not even four-foot end to end, it was shorter than Dean even. He looked down the row of dirt mounds that stretched beyond the pool of light created by the single bulb in the mechanic's lamp that hung from a loop of Romex that ran between two floor joists. Some mounds were longer than others. There were twelve by his count, though there were more stretching back into the shadows of the cellar that ran under the full footprint of the house above.

Dean set back to work, spading away at the hard-packed dirt while Sonny supervised, telling him to even up that side or give the hole more width. Once the older boy was satisfied, they worked together to drag the bundle to the hole and roll it in. Dean shoveled the fill back in from the pile he'd made by the grave.

"Shower's gonna feel good after this," Dean said. He was running with sweat, his face and arms caked with grit from digging.

"Dad says no shower for you," Sonny said. "Got a visitor comin' later."

Dean made a sour face. He knew who the visitor was, the sumbitch with the soft hands and hard eyes, the sumbitch who liked to give baths. Dean could smell the cheap cologne the man must have soaked in, the flowery stink of it invading his nose and mouth. Worse than that was the rancid odor of stale beer on his breath when he drew close to whisper in Dean's ear.

"Can I at least get a Coke when I come upstairs?"

"Soon's you're done," Sonny said, and rose with a grunt to go up the steps to the kitchen.

Left alone in the cellar, Dean moved the last of the earth to form a neat hill to match the others in the long row. With the blade of the shovel, he smoothed the dirt to create an even surface. He searched his mind as he patted the soil down, trying to recall the name of the boy he'd just buried. Try as he might, he couldn't remember the name even though he could swear he'd heard it said once or twice. He couldn't remember what the boy was called.

He leaned the shovel against the wall before snapping off the mechanic's lamp. He climbed the steps to the open doorway at the top, thinking of that ice-cold pop waiting for him upstairs. Thinking on that rather than what the evening ahead had to bring.

2

They gave the horses their head, letting the animals find their own way back to the stable and their feed buckets. The summer was nearly over, the scent of autumn already carried on the wind that was dropping down the ridgeline and on into the base of the holler. Even the sounds of the woods were changing. The rhythm of the cicadas was changing from an insistent chitter to a lazy rolling ambiance. Overhead, they could hear the honk of geese high in the sky, invisible through the cathedral ceiling of pine bowers.

"We had something we wanted to talk to you about, Daddy," Merry said. She was leaning back against the cantle of her western saddle, reins loose in her hand as Bravo, her chestnut gelding, picked his way down the slope.

"I thought we were just out for a ride," Levon said. He rode behind his daughter on an Appaloosa named Whiskey. It was a docile animal, dappled white over black with a pale blaze encircling one eye.

"We are," Hope said. The smaller girl was on a Welsh pony mare. She was named Penny for her reddish coat.

"A ride and a talk," Merry said.

"Sounds serious," he said.

"Well...it's about summer ending and..." Merry trailed off.

"Girl, what would Gunny say?"

"He'd say, 'Cut the bullshit'."

"Do what Gunny says."

"We want to go to school!" Hope blurted as she rode up even with Levon.

"School? Both of you?"

"Yes, Daddy," Merry said, turning on the saddle to look back at him. "This would be my last year in middle school and Hope's first, our last chance to be in the same school. I could look out for her."

"Depending on how Hope tested," Levon said.

"She'll test just fine. Her English is near perfect and she's reading at grade level. You should see her do math. She's better than me."

"This horse is better at math than you," her father said. Hope sniggered. "I thought you liked schooling at home."

"It's okay. But we don't meet many people way back up in here."

Levon knew that "people" meant boys, but didn't remark on that. His little girl was at that age, as much as he was loath to admit it.

"And how much does Sandy have to do with this?" he asked.

Sandy was Sandy Hamer, daughter of Jessie Hamer the local horse vet, and Merry's best friend aside from her new sister.

"Nothing besides telling us what Carson Creek School is like. Besides, she's at the high school. I wouldn't see her till next year."

"I'm gonna need to think about it," Levon said.

"That's not the code word for 'no' is it?" Merry said, reining back until he drew even.

"No. It means I'll have to think on how to make it work for the two of you. I'm gonna have to get paperwork for Hope. The paperwork will have to be good enough to stand up to the county looking hard at it."

"It is okay if only Merry goes to the school," Hope said behind them. "I can stay at home."

Levon shifted to look back at her. She was wearing the bravest little smile.

Esperanza Guzman was now Hope Cade but only according to some doctored adoption papers that would pass a cursory inspection. They'd never stand up to some curious school administrator willing to do some digging. Levon could get the proper documentation made up, but it would take money and time. The money was no problem, but he'd need to hustle to get an unassailable provenance for his new daughter in time for the first day of school.

"It's not gonna be a problem, honey. Just a little bit of thinking and working to make sure you're treated right."

Hope's smile became real with his words.

"So, that's 'yes'?" Merry said, her eyes narrowed at him.

"Yeah. I'll make it work," he said.

Merry let out a whoop.

"Come on, Hope," she said, spurring Bravo to a trot. "We need to pick out some clothes."

The girls took the horses into a canter and were soon

out of sight down the trail, leaving Levon to ride alone. Whiskey loped along, content with their easy pace and with no desire to chase after the younger cayuses. Levon only purchased the big lazy horse following months of Merry's pestering. He and his brother had ridden a bit when he was a kid, mostly to meet girls. Both had given it up when they realized that the horsey-set girls had their sights set higher than a pair of unreconstructed hillbillies. Levon and Dale went back to working on their cars and chasing the kind of girls who appreciated a boy with a hot set of wheels.

His riding skills came in handy during his time in Afghanistan, but that was all part of the job. Now, back home in the country he knew like an old friend, he had to admit that riding a horse was a relaxing experience. His renewed interest was due in no small part to his growing fondness for Jessie Hamer. Actually, she was a recently renewed interest, since they'd dated a time or two back in high school. He'd come full circle, he guessed. Back in the saddle because of the opposite sex.

Levon soon reached a broader section of trail that followed a shelf along the slope in a gentle curve down to the floor of the valley where Uncle Fern's acreage rested. From a section where the ground fell sharply away, Levon could see the house, barn, stables, and new garage building, the metal rooftops gleaming in the sun. Since coming home, he'd paid for improvements to the property, new roofs for all the buildings and the four-car garage, as well as an extension to the old house to add a bathroom for the girls and a screened-in porch.

Parked on the gravel of the yard were Levon's Avalanche and Uncle Fern's tricked-out Silverado. Next to them was a vehicle Levon didn't recognize, a beat-to-shit Ford pickup with a rusted bed and primer-shot cab. It could be one of Fern's old buddies from his days working thumpers and running white, but Levon knew all their rides.

He goosed Whiskey into a gallop. In his experience, it was best to greet bad news sooner than later.

3

The girls were already in the barn, brushing down their mounts when Levon led Whiskey in through the back gate of the paddock. He kept an eye out for Junebug, also known as Tricky Dick, the spotted goat that liked to ambush the unwary. He spotted the goat resting atop a stack of hay bales, content to watch the girls tending to the horses.

"Who's visiting?" he asked as he hauled the saddle and blanket off Whiskey.

"Don't know. We haven't been to the house yet," Merry said. She had Bravo cross-tied in the aisle between the stalls. She was working the loop of a steel-shedding comb over the dark coat.

"Take care of the horse and then yourself," Hope said with a smile. She was running water from a hose over her pony's legs, cooling the animal down.

"Then you don't mind taking care of Whiskey," Levon said and hitched the Appaloosa to a hoop bolted to a stall support.

"Daddy…" Merry sighed as he ducked under the crosslines and made for the barnyard.

"Remember the deal," he said. "I just ride. I don't put 'em up."

"Your father is funny," Hope said with a giggle.

"Oh, he's hilarious," Merry said with a crooked smile. "And he's your daddy now, too, you *pobre niña*."

The Ford parked in the yard looked even sadder on closer inspection. It had Alabama plates, a ball hitch crusty with rust, mismatched tires, and a side mirror hanging by a prayer from the passenger door. The rear window of the cab displayed an NRA sticker, a US Navy decal and another declaring that the truck was insured by Smith and Wesson. A large Yeti cooler that probably cost more than the heap's Blue Book value sat in the bed by a brand-new chrome tool bin.

Levon relaxed a bit as the dogs were resting quietly in the shade of the kitchen porch. His uncle's new dogs, a bluetick hound pup still growing into its paws and a feisty Jack Russell greeted him with wagging tails. The Russell, aptly named Rascal, jumped up to put front paws on his jeans legs until he ruffed the coarse fur on its neck.

He pulled open the screen door to step into the kitchen where Fern sat with a large man across the table, sharing a couple of long necks. Smoke from a Marlboro rested on the lip of a china saucer. It was cooler inside, but not by much. Levon had central air installed into the old place, but Fern didn't have it turned on most days, relying on a fly-specked old standing fan to move the air around.

The man at the table turned to greet Levon. He wore ripped and faded jeans and a clean white T-shirt with the sleeves rolled up tight to reveal arms covered to the wrists with ink—a map of Alabama, an unfurling Rebel battle flag, a woman wearing a pair of Daisy Dukes and not much else, and a skull with a rose in its grinning teeth. But the tat that drew his eyes was the jagged bolts of an SS emblem prominent on the visitor's forearm.

"You 'member me, Levon?" The man stood with a smile that revealed bright white implants next to teeth yellow as dried corn.

"Sure do, Teddy Lee." He stepped forward to take the man's offered hand. Edward Lee Cade was the youngest son of Fern's late cousin Billy. He'd know Teddy anywhere, even after all the time passed. He had the same piggy little brown eyes as when he was younger, but now they were framed by a pock-marked face fringed with a ginger beard that left his chin and upper lip clean. Teddy Lee was as big a man as his father was slight, just shy of Levon's 6'3", and swollen with prison muscle gone a bit soft since his release.

"It's just Lee now that Daddy's gone," Teddy said.

"Always be Teddy to me," Levon said, and they broke the handshake.

"That's cool. It is. You and me was always cool."

Levon could see the squared-off head of an eagle, beak sharply hooked, inked at the base of his cousin's throat. He knew that it topped black wings spread across Teddy's chest and ended with talons clutching a swastika just above the navel.

"We knew to give each other respect."

"King Kong and Godzilla." Teddy barked a wheezing laugh.

"Wendell and Alma told Teddy you were home from

the service," Fern said, getting up to pop the top of a beer for Levon.

"I was coming by anyway to visit Fern since he's been ill and such," Teddy said.

"I'm fine now. Gallbladder's out and so long as I avoid collards, I'm all fixed up," Fern said, handing the ice-cold beer to Levon before returning to his chair.

"All the way down from Murfreesboro to say hey?" Levon said, leaning back on the sink counter.

"I'm outside Birmingham these days," Teddy said. "But I get up here now and then. Got an ex over at Haley, works at the Walmart. She's management now."

"You still drop in on your ex?"

"We got kids together. Two girls close to your Merry's age, and a boy turned eight last month. I come up here once or twice a month to see them."

"Trying to be a good dad."

"Trying to be better than I was. No secret I been in trouble. Ran with a rough crowd, but I'm clean now." Teddy noticed Levon glancing at the beer in his hand. "I never had trouble with drink. Meth was a different story. I was deep into that shit too long. Cost me my family and a lot of years. I'm making up for that now."

"Good to hear," Levon said, the beer in his hand untouched and getting warm. Uncle Fern coughed into his fist.

"Teddy's having some trouble, Levon, with his boy Trevor."

"What kind of trouble?"

"He's gone. Didn't come home from school one day. Never got on the bus. No word, and this is the fifth day he's missing. Rowena's losing her mind over it."

"You mean Rowena Blanchard?"

"You remember her, do you?" A momentary gleam of pride in Teddy's eye.

"Hard not to."

"We were married just long enough to have three kids, two girls and then Trevor a couple years later. He's the baby."

"You go to the police about Trevor?"

"Police won't do shit. Them Haley cops is worse than useless and the staties won't touch it. They all say he's just run off."

"Could that be it? He just ran away? Doesn't sound right to me."

"No way. He's a little moody but what kid his age ain't moody? His life's good. Rowena makes good money and she's remarried now to a guy owns a Tire Kingdom. Trevor's got it better than I ever had, and I never took off."

"What do you want from me?" Levon asked.

"Help *finding* him, cousin," Teddy said. The big man's eyes were wetting up. He fought a sniffle with the back of his hand pressed under his nose.

"Why me?"

"You're some kind of badass war hero, ain't you? I mean, you could take a look around. Knock some heads together."

"You don't have friends?" Levon said, and gestured with the bottle at Teddy's arm.

"The Aryans? Nah, man, I can't associate with them. I have a PO who's a bitch on wheels. I go anywhere near them old boys and she'll violate me. I'm lucky to hold a job, she comes by so often to lookie-loo me."

"So, it's okay if I get in trouble."

"Like you ever walked away from trouble."

"Who told you about my military record?"

"Dale talked about you all the goddamn time. Listenin' to him, you were John Wayne, Rambo, and Chuck Norris all wrapped up together."

"My brother talked a lot of shit."

Teddy stood now, pushing back his chair.

"I wouldn't be asking you, but I'm out of moves. He's my *boy*. My blood. *Your* blood too. And, no bullshit, I'm scared of what might have happened to him. Who knows who he's with or who mighta taken him?"

"Will Rowena talk to me?"

"Sure, why not? I guess so. She'll remember you." The tension melted from Teddy's face.

"Give me her address," Levon said. "I'll go see her, see what she has to say. I'm no detective, Teddy. I can't promise you a thing."

"I don't want a detective, cousin. I need an ass kicker, and I'd do it myself only I'm afraid it would put me back in Bullock." Levon knew Teddy meant Bullock Correctional down in Union Springs.

"It's not like I have a Get Out of Jail Card myself."

"Just find him, Levon. Please, just do what you can," Teddy said and took Levon's hand in both of his.

4

"Garrett. Lone Star Solutions. How can I make your world a safer place?"

"You ever find out what they put in that *insarabasab* made us so sick?"

"Shit."

"Nice to talk to you too, buddy. What's all that shooting? You in the middle of something?"

"I'm at the range. Let me call you back on another phone."

"In five, okay?"

Tobey Garrett mimed apologies and walked away from the party of clients he was treating to an afternoon at Alamo Shooting Sports. They'd rented full-auto AKs and were running through enough ammo to max out his Amex, but if they hired him to watch over their truck depots, it would be worth it in spades.

"Cade, we are all paid up, even Steven," he said into a second phone as he paced between cars out in the parking lot.

"Can you really say a debt like that is really ever repaid?"

"You are a son of a bitch."

"And that's what it took to pull your ass out of the fire, a son of a bitch like me."

"Okay." Tobey sighed. "How much trouble are you gonna get me in now?"

"Just a referral, someone local. I need legitimate papers, identification, adoption, a full chain of solid bona fides."

"Local where?"

"Alabama. I'm back home, Tobey."

"How's that work? I thought every agency in the alphabet was after your ass."

"I got that straightened out. I have a clean bill of health now and all is forgiven."

"And here you are jumping into the shit again."

"Something I have to do. You know me."

"I sure as shit do, Cade."

Tobey gave out the name and location for the kind of help Levon Cade was looking for, then tabbed the call dead before opening his phone, snapping the SIM card in half, and crushing the phone under the heel of his Tony Lama.

———

The offices of Jay Morrison were in a strip mall in the Avondale section of Chattanooga. Levon sat in the air-conditioned reception area, sipping a black coffee after the two-hour drive up from Alabama. The receptionist, a middle-aged Black woman with a strong mothering instinct, asked him if he wanted the television on. He sensed that she was really asking for her own sake and said that he would. She aimed the remote and tabbed on a talk show with a smooth-talking male host with a N'awlins accent pretending to prepare a meal with a petite blonde in an apron and chef's hat. The audience was greatly amused by everything he said.

"That man is a darling," the receptionist said from her desk.

Levon nodded politely with no idea how he was supposed to respond to that. He was rescued when the door to a back office opened and a slender man with a reedy voice ushered an elderly couple across the lobby. The man wore a tailored Western-cut suit and cowboy boots. His hair was moussed back just so, and he had the hands of a concert pianist that fluttered before him in emphasis to his patter. He held the door for them to exit, all the while reassuring them that someone named Lonnie had no legitimate claim to their property and for them not to worry. Levon wondered if the receptionist thought her boss was also a darling.

"Are you Mr. Blackburn?" Morrison said as the door swung shut. He had a lazy Carolina drawl thick as syrup.

"That's me," Levon lied.

"Come on back then. Let's see if we can do anything for you."

The office was a windowless room with dark paneling and a wall of bookcases packed with neat rows of law volumes. Morrison's desk was a kidney-shaped slab of marble covered with stacks of files and sheaves of paper with a computer monitor sitting like an island in the middle.

"Do you have an electronic device on you, Mr. Blackburn?" the lawyer said.

"Am I wired?" Levon said.

"No one wears wires anymore. Do you have a recorder or smartphone?"

"No. Nothing like that."

"Okay then. What is it you're looking for? Need more coffee? Denisha can get you some."

Levon declined and presented Morrison with an envelope from his jacket containing some papers that included a birth certificate and photographs of Hope taken by Merry in front of a sheet tacked to a wall of their shared room. Hope wore a frozen smile in a white blouse with a Peter Pan collar.

"What a pretty little girl. Yours?" Morrison said as he placed reading glasses on his nose to inspect the documents.

"That's what I'm here for."

"This is very good," the lawyer said as he inspected the birth certificate. "It wasn't cheap, was it?"

"I'm willing to pay what it takes to get it right."

"What are you looking for then? How can I help you and your little one?"

"I need adoption papers that will stand up to scrutiny. I need a social security number and a hospital record and the social can't correspond to an existing owner. I don't want any identity theft here."

"Who'll be looking at this ID?"

"She's enrolling in school next week. The deadline is Thursday."

"That's ten days. That's manageable. Not to be indelicate, but this child looks Hispanic. Would she be an uninvited guest to this country?"

"Hope is an illegal. She came here under less than ideal circumstances, sir."

"I see," Morrison said, adjusting his glasses to peer closer at the birth certificate. "I also see that you have her birthplace as Knoxville. Will that be a problem?"

"Her English has come a long way in nine months," Levon said. "My daughter has her speaking fluent 'bama."

"That's just fine then. So, we're looking at $50,000.00 for documentation that's rock solid and unassailable, another $5,000.00 for me that's not part of the fifty, and my people may ask for another ten percent because of the tight deadline. That all sound like a plan to you, sir?"

"Half up front?" Levon took six packets of bills from a pocket of his jacket. They were hundreds bound with thick rubber bands.

The lawyer reached across the table to pick up a wad of the cash and held it to his nose.

"This will need to be laundered."

"Does that affect the cost?" Levon asked.

"I mean literally laundered, run through a washer. I might have gotten a contact high just touching these bills." With a chuckle, the lawyer scooped the bundles into an open drawer.

"Then something for wash day," Levon said and tossed another packet to the desktop.

"You are a true gentleman, Mr. Blackburn." Morrison smiled. "Or should I say, Mr. Cade?"

5

His mom never made it farther than the couch in the family room of their double-wide.

She lay totally sacked out, still in her uniform blouse from Denny's. The room smelled of fried potatoes and onions. He knew she was down till late in the day.

Russ made do with a Pop-Tart for breakfast. He slipped from the house with it clenched in his teeth and ate it as he rode his bike through the morning quiet streets of the subdivision. There was no one outside but a guy tearing down a riding mower on his driveway. The basketball court was empty. No kids splashed in the Martinson's above-ground pool.

He hated to admit it, but Russ was kind of glad summer was almost over. His first day of eighth grade was less than a week away and he realized he was looking forward to it. There were kids he was anxious to meet up with again, and he hadn't seen Kathy Higgins since the last day of school, being that she lived over in Towpath on the other side of the state road. He wondered if she still wore her hair long. He vowed to himself that this year, *this* year, he'd try and talk to her.

Close to three months of idleness, staying up late, sleeping late, had left him bored. He thought about pedaling over to Dougie's house to play Xbox, but Dougie only ever wanted to play that stupid racing game and Russ wanted to *shoot* something. Russ wanted his own Xbox, and his mother told him he could have one if he'd gotten "off his lazy ass and got a summer job".

Russ coasted down the long hill and followed the curving lane to the subdivision entrance for the county road. He turned right and stayed in the bike lane to the collection of stores down where the county road crossed the pike to a Walgreens, a Popeye's, a shuttered hardware store, and a Shell station with a mini-mart.

There was no one he knew hanging out. Come school days, the front of the mini-mart would be crowded with kids before and after classes. A fresh, new *ONLY 2 STUDENTS AT A TIME* sign was taped up on the glass of one of the double doors. He leaned his bike against the storefront where he could see it from inside while he bought an iced tea. Outside, Russ popped the top of the tall can and thought about cruising down the pike to the bowling alley, only he remembered he didn't have any money for the arcade. He drifted across the lot, not sure which direction he'd take.

"Hey, you go to Weatherford?" A kid a couple years older than him was filling a Nissan pickup out by the pump island.

"Yeah," Russ said and turned to circle back to the pumps.

"Thought I'd seen you 'round," the other kid said. Skinny kid with surfer hair in a sleeveless tee that showed off a tattoo of a cross on one bicep. It was bluish and poorly done. Russ had seen the kid around before but couldn't remember his name.

"Me too. Going into ninth this year."

"I'm starting seventh," Russ said. He'd seen this kid before at the bowling alley, never at school. Russ remembered him because he always seemed older than his age.

"Cool. One more week of freedom, huh?"

"Yeah."

"You live around here?"

"In Bowling Green Commons, back up that way." Russ gestured with his head back to the county road.

"Bored off your ass, right?" The kid replaced the nozzle on the pump and twisted the gas cap in place.

"Shit, yeah."

"Same here. Last week of summer and I done everything I wanted, seen all the movies, felt up all the girls."

Russ sniggered in agreement at that and thought of Kathy Higgins, remembering her in the cafeteria, hanging with her girl posse. Thinking about the time he sat across the table from her at the library, the way her violet-colored eyes moved as she read the book open in front of her.

"Hey," the other kid said. "If you could do anything you wanted right now, what would you do?"

"I dunno," Russ said. "Anything in the world?"

"In the world."

"I'd play some Xbox, but the only kid I know has one only wants to play *Ridge Racer*."

"And you want to shoot some shit up."

Russ shrugged and grinned.

"Well, hell, son. We got Xbox at our house. Come on

back with me. We got *Assassin's Creed, Red Dead, Mass Effect*, all the good shit. We'll go to war together."

"Maybe, I guess."

"Then let's go. Throw your bike in the back," the kid said and got in the cab behind the wheel.

"Bullshit. You're not sixteen. You don't drive."

"I wouldn't shit you," the kid said with an easy smile. "My dad's disabled. Got a special driver's license so I can cart his ass around." He pointed a finger at a blue sticker on the windshield that featured the white outline of a wheelchair.

"I guess it'd be okay then."

"You need to call home first?"

"Nah. My mom works nights. She's asleep. Don't have a phone on me anyway."

The kid's smile broadened.

"Then toss that bike in the back and we'll get our asses outta here."

Russ dropped the tailgate to slide his bike under the tonneau cover and onto the bed. The back of the truck was empty but for a couple of cases of beer empties. He raised and secured the tailgate in place before joining the kid in the cab. The kid had lit a Marlboro that bled smoke between the fingers of a hand resting easy atop the steering wheel.

"What kind of disabled is your dad?" Russ asked as the truck turned out onto the pike, making a left and heading west.

"Nothing you can see," the kid said. "But he's all fucked up *inside*, y'know?"

"It gonna be okay, me comin' over like this?"

"It's gonna be fine, m'man." Sonny smiled from behind the wheel. "I gotta feeling he'll like you."

6

Levon took the exit for Haley on the way home. He thought about calling Rowena Cade, now Abruzzi, before showing up. But, true to his word to Morrison he had no smartphone or cell phone of any kind. It had never occurred to him that every payphone on the planet had vanished along with mailboxes and TV aerials. He really needed to pick up a cell phone.

He decided to show up cold. This was about her missing son, after all.

The house was on a cul-de-sac at the end of a street called Cherokee Court in a gated development named Keowee Creek. Levon didn't see any creeks in the winding maze of manicured lawns and mini-mansions, and he for sure saw no Cherokees other than a Jeep parked in a driveway next to a Maybach sedan.

His cousin's former wife lived in a red brick house set well off the street at the end of a paving stone driveway that ended at a three-car garage. It was for certain better than whatever shit-box Teddy had provided her when they were married. He rang the doorbell set in a frame next to tall double doors with inset beveled glass panels. There was no sign of movement through the prismatic glass, so he pressed the bell again.

"Hold on, y'all, dammit!" came a shout from somewhere within. You can take the girl out of the holler, but you can't take the holler out of the girl.

Rowena Abruzzi hauled the door wide and squinted into the sunlight at the tall stranger standing on her walk. She was barefoot in stretch pants and a loose-fitting pullover with a low collar that offered a generous view of the curve of her breasts. Her dyed indigo hair was short cropped. A stray strand hung over one eye and danced with the movement of her brows.

"And you are?" she said, hipshot in the doorway.

"Teddy Lee might have told you I'd be stopping by."

"Well, goddamn to Hell! Levon Cade!" Her defiant stance melted away in a broad, full-lipped smile.

"I remember you too, Rowena."

"Not like this, huh? You knew me when, before I had my teeth straightened and boobs beeped up." She laughed at her own remark and stepped aside for him to enter.

Levon took a seat at the edge of a leather chair in a family room at the center of the open plan cavern that formed the core of the house. To be polite, he accepted Rowena's offer of an iced tea. She sat on the couch with something clear on ice in a squared-off tumbler.

"Don't know how much Teddy told you. This ain't the first time Trevor's taken off," Rowena said, the ice making a musical sound against the glass as she gestured with it. "He was away close to a week when I married Victor. Rebellion, I guess. He's a smart kid but kinda moody; not sure where he got *that*." The sarcasm was thick in her voice.

"Where was he the week he was gone?"

"His friend's house, some runt he plays those stupid games with, you know, with dragons and elves and shit."

"What's this other kid's name?"

"Del. Del Washington. The kids all call him Wash. Lives over in Tall Pines."

"You talked to this other kid, Rowena? Does he know where Trevor might be?"

"I sent Victor over there to ask. The kid don't know nothing. Says he was looking for Trevor on the bus the day Trevor didn't come home."

"Could he be lying? Maybe Trevor's over at his house right now."

"Nah. Victor says the kid seemed scared and his mom backed him, said Trev hadn't been around there."

"What about his sisters? Two older girls, right?"

Rowena blew through her lips to make a dismissive sound.

"It's like they ain't even in the same family or on the same planet. Those girls are more likely to talk to the dog than to their little brother."

"What did the police tell you?"

"The usual cop bullshit. Two staties saying they'll do all they can and keep us updated and no one will rest until Trevor's found and all that noise while they don't do jack dick."

"You have to give them time, Rowena."

"That's all they got, is time. I seen 'em parked at the Waffle House hours on end." She set her glass down on an end table with a bang that splashed liquor on her hand.

Levon sat forward, eyes idly scanning the covers of magazines on the glass-topped coffee table between them—*Garden and Gun, Southern Living, People.*

"So, what will you do now, Levon?" Rowena was resting back on the sofa with her feet under her, tapping a ring on the tumbler. Her eyes swam a bit under heavy lids. Her smile was more crooked now. This tumbler wasn't her first drink of the day.

"I'm not sure. I told Teddy I'm not a cop."

"But you're a smart one, always were. Smartest one in that crowd you ran with, though that ain't saying a *whole* lot."

"Maybe I should take a look at his room. That's what the detectives on TV do, right?"

"Well, come on up then," she said, and uncurled herself from the sofa to lead the way up the steps.

The boy's room was like any other, but with more expensive toys maybe. A bookcase was filled with stacks of comic books and action figures. A Crimson Tide comforter was on the twin bed, a gift from his stepdad, Levon guessed. There were posters taped to the wall— fantasy stuff, monsters, women warriors, and medieval settings. The room was neat and organized. Levon surmised that Rowena had help in. She sure wasn't cleaning toilets dressed as she was.

At the center of a desk was an open laptop, the screen dark.

"He do a lot on the computer?" Levon said.

"Lives on it," Rowena said from where she leaned in the doorway.

"So why's it here? Why didn't he take it to school?"

"He's got a phone does all the things that does. He only uses the laptop for schoolwork and his games."

"Would it be okay if I took it along with me?" Levon asked.

"Sure, I guess so." She shrugged. "Not sure what you'll find on there that'll help you, just a lot of that elf shit. Sometimes I wish he watched porn; you know, something normal?"

"I'll have someone look at it and bring it back soon's I can," Levon said as he pressed the laptop closed and pulled the power cord from an outlet set in the desktop. There were stickers depicting cartoon robots on the lid.

"He has a passcode. I'll need that. Any ideas?" Levon asked.

"He keeps it written on a sticky note there."

Levon plucked a yellow Post-it from where it was stuck to the bell of a desk lamp. Letters and numbers were written neatly in black ink—*b1gg3r0nth31ns1d3*

"It's from some stupid show he watches." Rowena was leaning a shoulder against the doorjamb, blocking his exit. Her long, manicured fingers played up and down the sweating surface of the tumbler in her hands.

"You don't need to rush off in such a hurry, do you? I'm not due at work till later. Evening shift," she said. Her eyelids drooped lower, the tip of her tongue visible in the corner of her smile.

"It'd be better if I got back home."

"Why? You ain't married. I see you wear a wedding ring, but I heard your wife passed a while back."

"You're married, Rowena."

"*Happily* married," she declared. "Victor's a good man. He treats me right. He's not like Teddy. Not at all, uh uh. Vic knows how to use his hands. Got gentle hands, that boy. You know what I'm talking about?"

"I really need to go, Rowena."

"You remember that Legion picnic we was on? Fourth of July, down at the lake?"

Levon said nothing in reply.

"We both come out of the woods soaking wet." Her eyes darkened at the memory. "Folks was joking that you pushed me into the lake, and I pulled you in after, only neither of us was in the water once that day."

"I really need to go, Rowena. Thanks for the tea."

"Can't blame a girl for trying," she said with a wincing smile, and stepped back into the hallway to allow him through. "You can find your own way out."

As he walked down the stairs for the front door, the laptop under his arm, she leaned over the railing to call after him.

"You always *was* a stiff prick, Levon Cade. Guess that's why I liked you back then."

When the door closed and Levon was gone, Rowena returned to Trevor's room. She idly straightened some of the stuff that sat atop his dresser. There were framed pictures of him alone and with his sisters, a funny one of his first Halloween when he went around the trailer park where they lived then, dressed as a puppy dog. She glanced at the space atop his desk where the laptop rested a few moments before.

With a mind of its own, her hand picked up a plastic figure from the desk, an ugly as sin cartoonish monster with an outsized head and tiny body. She took a seat on the edge of his bed, holding the figure in her hands, trying to remember the name of it. This kind of stuff, this silly stuff, was important to her little boy but she never paid the slightest bit of attention to any of it.

She tossed the figure across the room as the tears came. They came for a long while, not stopping until she heard the bang of the front door opening and the voices of her girls filling the first floor.

7

"An eight-year-old boy's computer?" Jessie Hamer said. "God alone knows what we're about to see here."

"Rowena said he's not into anything nasty," Levon said, seated on a barstool next to her. The laptop sat open on a serving counter in Jessie's kitchen. Jessie tapped in the password off the yellow Post-it.

"Nasty as she is," Jessie snorted.

"You remember her from school?"

"I should say I do. Biggest whore around, as if you don't know."

Levon said nothing. Jessie turned to him, eyes narrowed.

"She came *on* to you! Do not even *try* to lie to me, Levon."

"She might have made a few suggestions."

"Well, you're gonna have to tell me *all* about that when we're done here." Jessie shifted her hips on her seat and moved a finger over the touchpad.

The screen came to life with a garish image of two costumed characters fighting one another high above a city skyline. Jessie moved the cursor to open a menu densely populated with programs. She opened Google Chrome and found the browsing history.

"You do this on Sandy's computer?" he said.

"Spy on my daughter?" Jessie laughed as she dove deep into Trevor Cade's cyber life. "All the damn time, on her tablet, her phone, the car. You do the same on Merry, right?"

"I guess I should. Seems like a violation of our trust."

"Get over yourself. As much trouble as your little one's found herself in, I wonder why you don't have a microchip put on her. You know, I'm a vet. I could do that. You want me to chip Merry?"

"Maybe for her birthday. You seeing anything I can use?"

"Maybe on his Facebook. You can spend some time with that yourself. There's a couple of private message boards he belongs to, too but what Rowena told you is right. Looks like he's into gaming and fantasy stuff, Japanese cartoons and like that. I don't see how this stuff can help you much."

"I keep telling everyone I'm not a detective."

"You know people though, don't you? People you could reach out to?"

"I'm trying to leave all that behind. My favor bank is overdrawn as it is. I'm gonna try to do what I can here without outside help."

"I can understand that," Jessie said. "But there's only so much you can learn here. It's not like he posted where he took off to."

"If he had a say in that."

"You think it's that bad," she said, turning to at him.

"Hard to say. There's too many unanswered questions."

"You thought of talking to his friends, this Wash kid?"

"I have no authority, Jess. I have no right asking these kids questions. How would you feel if some stranger came around wanting to talk to Sandy about her school friends?"

"Yeah. I see."

"Can you show me the Facebook and the message boards?" Levon moved off the stool to stand behind her to watch what she did on the screen. The passwords to each site were saved in the cloud and easily accessed.

"Look, I'll bookmark them. You can find them here at the bottom of the list. Once you're on the sites, it's all pretty intuitive. You really don't know how to do this stuff, do you?"

"I've been a bit out of touch living in the real world. But this is intelligence gathering, right?"

"You did some of that during your time in service?"

"Usually I was just acting on intel others found, but as often as they screwed it up, I couldn't do much worse."

"There. You're all set," she said and closed the laptop before swiveling the chair around to face him. He remained where he was, a hand touching her knee.

"You stop anywhere on the way back from Haley?" she said. "I could fix you some lunch."

"I had a late breakfast." He looked down at her, touching his fingers to a feather of stray hair that had come free from a barrette at her temple.

"Well, then," she said, rising from the chair to step

into his arms. "Maybe you can tell me more about these suggestions Rowena was making to you."

————

Levon stood, tucking his work shirt back into his jeans. Jessie lay back in the queen-size bed in her master bedroom. She was propped against pillows, the sheet pulled over her naked body.

"How's Whiskey handling for you?" she asked, sitting up, a hand brushing her loose hair back.

"I don't want to ask what brought that up right about now," he said.

"You have a filthy mind, cowboy."

"Whiskey is just fine. His temperament suits me. I think we have an understanding and it's good riding with the girls. You should see Hope on that pony; a natural, that little one." He tugged his belt closed and sat on the edge of the bed by her.

Jessie swung her bare legs to the floor and snuggled closer to him, only the fabric of the sheet between them. The afternoon sun through the bay windows revealed stray strands of silver along her temples. He leaned over to kiss her just above the ear. They sat that way for a while, enjoying the shared peace.

"I'd better go. You said Sandy would be home soon," Levon said, making to rise.

"Now you've got a guilty conscience," she said and poked him in the ribs before clutching his arm tighter, drawing him back down beside her.

"What's she gonna think, Jess, coming home and finding me and you here alone?"

"I think she suspects something already."

"You think she's told Merry? Those two tell each other everything."

"You're worried what your little girl will think. Are you ashamed of me?" But Jessie was smiling.

He turned and pressed her back on the bed, leaning on an elbow beside her. His fingers played with the hem of the sheet held above her breasts. She tightened her grip on the sheet, giggling as she squirmed under him.

"I could never be ashamed of you, Jess, and Merry loves you, you know that. I just don't want to have to answer a lot of questions, is all."

"What kind of questions?"

"You know what kind of questions little girls ask."

"Same as big girls, I'd guess."

"You know. 'When you gonna get married' and like that."

"Well?" Jessie looked him in the eye, a brow raised.

"Well, what?" He turned his head to look at her askance.

"How would you answer that?"

"You mean, if we're gonna get married?"

"You said 'when', Levon. You said *when* we're gonna get married."

"I did, didn't I?"

She canted her head, eyes still fixed on him, both brows raised now.

"Okay, then," he said. "But that's something a guy asks with roses and a ring and all that."

"Too late," Jessie said and pulled the sheet aside to wrap her arms around the back of his neck and pull herself closer for a lingering kiss.

———

Sandy Hamer brought her Kia to a stop in the drive. Mr. Cade's truck was parked there by her mom's work truck. As she stepped from the car, she could hear a peal of her mother's laughter. It was coming through the open bay window on the second floor. Sandy rolled her eyes, standing for a moment with her hand on the door of the car. She eased the door shut and walked across the drive to the stables where she took off her sneakers and slipped on a pair of Wellies.

The stalls needed mucking; she'd do it now rather than after dinner. Let her mom keep her little game of pretend going, acting like nothing was going on with Mr. Cade.

She would make sure to be there when Mr. Cade came out. She'd let out a big old hello and watch his neck turn red. Sandy wouldn't miss that for the world.

8

Russ didn't know where he was or how he got there.

He woke on an unfamiliar bed in a room with a wall-paper of ugly red flowers wrapped in green vines against a field of faded black. There were square places where the flowers were more richly colored, places where framed pictures once hung. The ceiling above him had a crack running the length of it. He looked at the crack a long time, trying to focus thoughts that wouldn't come together. He thought about getting up, leaving the bed. His body was slow to respond to his thoughts, as if his hands and feet were a million miles away.

After a month or so, he managed to rise to a sitting position. A week later, he swung his legs off the edge of the bed. In another few days, his feet touched the worn area rug in the center of a pale wood floor. He realized for the first time that his feet were bare. Someone had taken his sneakers and socks. His clothes were gone too. His cargo shorts and Batman T-shirt were replaced with loose-fitting pajamas several sizes too large for him. In the back of his dulled mind, a tingle of fear came to life.

The room was in an older house, Russ could tell. The bed was an old iron four-poster. The only other furniture in the room was a battered chest of drawers painted a pale blue that was peeling now. One of the drawers had a brass lock set in its face.

Ornate wooden molding ran along the foot of the walls and around the edges of the ceiling. The light in the ceiling was a single bulb in a cut glass fixture covered in a greasy coat of dust. The light was out now, the only source of illumination coming from the gap in the blackout curtains that hung from the room's only window.

On unsteady feet, Russ made his way the mile or so to the window and pulled back one of the curtains. It was full dark out, hours after he'd left the Shell station with…what was his name again? The light outside was from a pole lamp that sat at the edge of a parking area of cracked asphalt and gravel before a shake-sided garage building. There were bars bolted to the outside of the window. Wrought iron like the ones around the yard of a neighbor back in the subdivision. The tingle of fear sparked to life again.

There was no light to be seen anywhere else, no other houses, just trees all around. No road or highway sounds, just the rising and falling chirrup of toads. He let go of the curtain and stepped back, his vision going gray then black.

Russ next came awake on the floor, not remembering falling. He lay there, watching shadows play across the single bar of light that shone on the ceiling from the open space in the curtains. The shadows were from moths fluttering around the bare bulb of the pole lamp outside, their forms projected large on the plaster above his head.

Russ rolled to his side and got to his feet with a great deal of effort. He shuffled to the door and tried the knob. It turned but did not release the lock. There were metal plates along the edge of the door above the knob and he could see the bolts of heavy locks in the narrow gap between the door and the frame. He slid to the floor by the door to sit with his back to it.

His memories of how he came to be here wafted in and out of his mind's eye. The long ride from the Shell station, west along the pike through open fields, then a cutoff into some woods, the road turning from paved to unpaved past a trailer park. The road rose to higher ground, the woods turning to dense evergreen forest. Sonny, that was his name, talked the whole time, though Russ couldn't recall one thing he said. All he knew was that the boy at the wheel made him laugh.

The unpaved road turned to crushed gravel before ending at a big house of green shakes. Two stories and some additions off the side and back. The garage building he saw from the window was back off the rear of the house. There was a car and another pickup out front of the house, and a motorcycle sat under a tarp in a carport. Sonny said something about the motorcycle, but Russ either didn't understand or forgot what he said.

Inside, the house smelled like bacon grease and cigarettes. It was darker inside than out, heavy curtains covering the windows of every room. Sonny led Russ to a room at the back. They passed other rooms on the way that lined a long hallway that ran alongside a staircase to the second floor. One door was closed with a heavy deadbolt lock set in place. Sonny noticed Russ paying attention to the locks.

"Dads keeps all his good stuff in there," Sonny said. "He don't like us foolin' with any of his stuff."

Dads. Who was Dads?

They came to a broad archway and through it to a large room lined on one wall with windows covered with thick curtains. There were a pair of sofas set at angles to one another and facing a large-screen TV. A boy a year or so younger than Russ lay on one of the sofas watching cartoons, a bowl filled with dry cereal lay by his side. He was eating with his fingers.

"Dean, get that shit off. We're gonna play some games," Sonny said.

The boy sat up then and aimed the remote to kill the screen and bring the room to silence.

"You hungry, Russ? I can make us sandwiches. Peanut butter and raisins okay?" Sonny said.

"Peanut butter and jelly if you got it."

"The classic. Sure. I'll bring Cokes too," Sonny said, stepping back into the hallway. "Dean, show our guest where the games are kept. Russ, pick out one you want to play."

The younger boy pulled a cardboard box out from beside the cabinet the TV rested on. It was packed with row after row of game boxes. Russ began looking through them for a first-person shooter.

"You and Sonny brothers?" Russ asked.

"We are now," Dean answered.

By the time Russ picked out a game and set it by the console, Sonny had returned with a tray. There were sandwiches sliced in neat halves on two paper plates along with a bowl of chips and two cans of Coke. They were both already opened. Russ took his sandwich and drank while Sonny placed the game in the console and set the TV the way they needed it. Sonny handed him the controller and promised to go easy on him the first time.

Russ could remember starting the game, eating the sandwich thick with peanut butter and strawberry jam. He took sips from the soda to wash it down. After some time, he began to lose interest in the game. Russ noticed Sonny watching him, dividing interest between the game and keeping an eye on him. It became harder and harder to find the proper buttons on the controller. They seem to shift in his vision as though someone were trying to pull the controller from his hands.

Russ felt his attention wandering, his eyes roaming away from the action on the screen and around the room. Dean, the younger boy, sat on the other sofa studying Russ with detached interest. He said something to Sonny, but the words sounded far away like from the end of a tunnel. Russ braced a hand on the arm of the sofa and tried to rise. He turned his head past Sonny who was smiling at him, amused, to see a small figure standing at the edge of the archway that led to the hall. A little boy, a Black boy with a close-cropped afro and jug ears, maybe six, maybe seven years old. The boy was watching Russ, dark eyes fixed on him.

The last thing he could recall with any clarity was what the Black child was wearing. It was a Halloween costume, the kind his mom used to buy him at Walmart when he was little. This one was blue and white and had a picture of a cartoon pony on the front.

And then, things went black. And then, he woke up in the room with the flowered walls.

Russ sat up when he heard a metallic click above his head, followed by another. The bolts in the locks were being drawn back. He slid away from the door as it swung open and Sonny was standing there, balancing a tray on one arm.

"Thought you'd still be in the bed," Sonny said, entering the room and pulling the door closed behind him. He set the tray atop the dresser and came back to help Russ to his feet. He guided Russ to a sitting position on the bed.

"It's late. I need to call my mom," Russ said. His voice came as a whispering croak and that surprised Russ.

"You don't like it here?" Sonny smiled. "No school. No chores. Watch TV and play games all the time?"

"She'll be worried."

"Moms like to worry. That's why they do it all the time." Sonny went to the dresser and returned with a tall glass filled with something thick. Russ took the glass in his hands. It was ice cold to the touch.

"I'm not so hungry," he said.

"Sure, you are. Just a little woozy. This milkshake'll make that go away," Sonny said, returning to the tray on the dresser. He held out a little paper cup. It had an oblong pill the color of school chalk inside.

"What's that?" Russ said.

"It'll make it so it don't hurt so much," Sonny said and tipped the pill into Russ's hand. His smile had become brittle now, and there was a change in his eyes as he regarded Russ.

Russ started to ask what was going to hurt but could not form the words. The hot tingle of fear became an icy cold stabbing sensation in the pit of his stomach.

He could not ask because he did not want to know.

9

"That shit'll rot your mind, nephew," Uncle Fern said as he tapped grinds from his coffee maker into the trash.

"How would you know that?" Levon said.

Levon had Trevor's laptop open on the kitchen table and was in no mood for comments. He'd found the laptop virtually useless until Merry had shown him how to hook the machine up to the satellite provider she and Hope used. She gave him the passwords that would allow him to access the router in her room and therefore the network she'd set up.

"Where did you learn this stuff?" he had asked her.

"I just know it, Daddy. It's easy."

Now Fern was busting his balls, an old man who still had a dial phone on his kitchen wall.

"I saw it on Tucker," Uncle Fern said. "He talks about it all the time, how this social media and Twitter crap is turning us all into zombies." Fern was a devoted watcher of Tucker Carlson. To Levon's uncle, the preppy Yankee was practically a seer.

"Well, this is business," Levon said.

"You mean Teddy Lee's paying you?" Fern said, measuring fresh grounds into his percolator.

"Family business."

Fern made a *phah* sound and flipped a switch on the ancient brewer. It began bubbling away and filling the kitchen with the scent of fresh java.

"Why don't you throw that old piece of junk away and let me buy you a new coffee maker?" Levon said.

"One of those gadgets you put the little plastic cups in?" Fern said with a face. "They had one of them at the oil change place. Stuff tasted like watered-down cow shit."

"Well, you don't talk to me about computers, and I won't talk to you about how you make that nasty mud you drink."

Levon returned his attention to the laptop screen while Fern took his Marine bulldog coffee mug to the living room to watch a Western. The Jack Russell trotted behind him, nose up to sniff for the plate of sandwich cookies Fern took along to go with the coffee.

Levon was surprised to see that it was close to three in the morning when he finally looked up from the laptop. Nearly four hours had passed and he knew little more about his second cousin than he did before. Trevor had about thirty friends on his social media page. Most of them were only a certain brand of stranger, and most all of them boys his age. Only a few of them were local. There were kids he exchanged posts and messages with from other countries. There were only two girls, one from Russia and the other from Ukraine, and they were clearly phonies. Their posts and replies were laughably crude and non sequitur. But Levon gathered that Trevor was aware of this and only stayed in contact to see the near-naked pictures they posted of themselves.

There was no one in his group that raised any suspicion. Levon could tell from private messages that he actually knew the local boys he was communicating with. There were no adults posing as children aside from the Russian bots, no new acquaintances suggesting they meet in person. Most of the exchanges, posts, and direct messages were between Trevor and The Mighty Lord of Doom who turned out to be his friend, Wash. They talked about games, comic books, upcoming movies and, on rare occasions, girls. Even then, it was about actresses on TV that they both found attractive.

The same held true for his email account. Most of the communications were with Wash and another boy named Brian. Brian lived in the same development as Trevor and went by slashmaster196 on Facebook. He was two years older than Trevor and from the traffic between them, they were drifting apart. The Slashmaster had probably discovered the opposite sex over the summer, Levon guessed.

And Rowena was right—the nearest her son came to pornography was a file in documents labeled "homework, etc." which was filled with various image files of Scarlett Johansson in some kind of skintight costume.

All in all, if this device offered an honest glimpse into the boy's life, then he was just the average nerdy kid picked last for sports. There was no sign of the reckless habits of a risk-taker. The most outrageous thing Trevor had done was to try vaping last spring at the insistence of a couple of kids from his class. He confessed to Wash in a DM that he threw up for the rest of the day. He had to tell his mother it was something he ate at school and she called the school dietitian and gave the woman hell. There were many LOLs shared over that one between the two boys.

A perfectly uneventful life and a good kid who did well in school and followed the rules.

None of that was good news in the face of Trevor's disappearance.

It meant the boy had an unintended misadventure.

It meant something bad. Levon began to feel time pressing down on him.

10

The heavy tread of feet in the hallway awakened Russ.

He raised his head from the pillow as, one by one, the locks on the door opened with an oiled snick. It was hard to lift his head and sit up. He was a little dizzy. He couldn't remember ever sleeping that hard.

The door swung open and a man entered, a man older than his dad, bigger, too. A man with a broad face and wide shoulders and a paunch that stretched his golf shirt to hang over his belt in a roll. The shirt had some kind of sports logo embroidered on the breast. His hair looked wet and slicked back. There was a smell that came into the room with him, flowers and pine.

"You awake enough to listen to me?" the man said as he went to the dresser to rattle a key in the brass lock of the top drawer.

"Yes, sir," Russ said, his voice sounding far away.

"'Sir.' I like that. I do. You're gonna do fine here." The man rooted around in the drawer and laid several objects on the dresser top. They looked like toys almost. Colorful and made of plastic or rubber.

"I want to go home. I want to see my mom," Russ said. He heard the quaver in his throat. He realized that he sounded afraid. Funny, the fear was in his voice but not his heart or mind.

"No can do, little man," the big man said. He stepped across the room to take Russ's hand and pull him to sitting position. He sat next to Russ, an arm around him. The flowers and pine scent became stronger in Russ's nostrils. They sat close enough that Russ could see the sheen of sweat on the man's face. He could read the logo on the golf shirt. A team logo of a cartoon wolf snarling. Above it was embroidered the name "Dads." The man was smiling now, showing teeth.

"My mom will be worried about me."

"That'll pass, son. She'll move on. Just like you've moved on."

Russ sniffed, hot tears welling in his eyes.

"None of that now," the big man cooed. "You're gonna like it here. Nothing to do but play games and watch the TV. No school. No one to tell you to go to bed. You're free to do what you like."

"Then I want to leave."

"That's the one thing you can never do, little man," the big man said. The smile froze on his face like it took real effort to keep it there.

"You have to let me leave."

"Listen to me." The man's voice dropped deeper, and he spoke barely above a whisper. "You even try to get out of this house, you even think of leaving here and I will kill your mom. You hear me? You step one foot out this house and your mom is dead."

The clouds in Russ's mind parted with those words.

He stared into the eyes of the big man. What he saw there made him believe the man's promise.

"She done nothing to you." His voice rose higher with each word.

"That's right, little man. You mom did nothing wrong, but she'll die anyway. And it won't be me killing her. It'll be you. So, you do as you're told, and your mom will be just fine, safe as safe can be. But you have to be a good little man. You understand what I'm telling you, do you?"

Russ nodded.

The man reached out with big fingers and pulled the lids of one of Russ's eyes wide open. Then he reached into a pocket of his pants and took out an amber bottle from the drug store. He handed Russ a white pill the same as he'd taken earlier. Was that yesterday? Last night?

"You take this. Chew it up and swallow it. It'll help."

Russ did as he was told. The pill was chalky and bitter. The grit scratched his throat as it went down.

The man went to the dresser and came back to the bed with one of the toys that wasn't a toy.

"Faster you learn, the sooner you can come downstairs with the other boys. Now you do as I say, little man, we'll all get along just fine."

The big man took a fistful of Russ's hair in a huge hand. The world turned pink around the edges as the drug he swallowed took effect.

Sonny lied.

It hurt.

11

"You know we have an intercom, Diane," Sheriff Elmo Struthers said to his administrative assistant standing before his desk.

"It's the Loomis woman again," Diane was frustrated. "She's been calling two days now and I'm running out of pat phrases."

"It's almost the end of the day." Elmo sighed. "Field this one last call for me, all right?"

"She's not on the phone, sheriff," Diane said. "She's in the waiting area."

"Shit."

"I'll show her in then." Diane stepped back to the office door and beckoned to someone in the squad room.

Carline Loomis brushed past Diane. She wore a blouse with the Denny's logo over one breast, white sneakers, and dark slacks. She was an attractive woman by the sheriff's standards, if a little worn around the edges. From the scent of bacon off her, he guessed she'd driven down here to the county seat right after the breakfast shift ended.

"Sheriff, I hate havin' to come down here like this," she said, taking a stand on the carpet as he stood up to greet her. "But all I'm gettin' is runaround and bullshit from your deputies."

"I am sorry, Ms. Loomis, and I am aware of your son's case. I cannot imagine…"

"Yeah. Yeah. Bullshit, Sheriff." Carline made a karate chop motion to shut him down. "Everyone's sorry. Everyone feels bad. I had enough of that. My Russell's gone almost two days now and we're comin' up on the weekend, and I'm getting' nothin' but everybody's prayers and thoughts. Good vibes ain't gonna get the job done."

"I have two detectives on it now."

"I talked to them. I'm surprised they found their way back to their car. Kept on and on about drugs. My boy doesn't do drugs. He knows I'd kick his ass."

"Stivers and Breem are fine investigators, Ms.—"

"Bullshit and *bull* shit." The karate chop again. "It's a little boy. He's gone. No one saw nothin'. He was *taken*. Isn't this an FBI thing?"

"There's no evidence that this was a kidnapping. No ransom demand."

"It's my little boy," Carline said. Tears gave her eyes a silvery gleam under the ceiling fluorescents.

"I've spoken to the county district attorney. He's asking State CID for help with this. We're asking for help from the churches and schools to search the woods near your house."

"Then you think he's dead."

"I didn't say that, Ms. Loomis."

"He knows his way home from the woods. You're sayin' he *can't* come home."

"Please, Ms. Loomis." He came around the desk to take her arm and guide her to a seat in his visitor's chair. "Diane! Get me a coffee for Ms. Loomis."

The sheriff shared his box of tissues with the woman who collapsed in tears, head lying on an arm on his desk. He felt for her. He truly did. He had three kids of his own, only they were all grown now. He also felt his lack of power, his inability to make truth of his promises. He had ten deputies to cover a big county. The population was sparse, but they had their share of crime. Highest per capita population of formerly and currently incarcerated citizens in the state of Alabama. Murders, thefts, robberies, and burglaries all driven by the meth and oxy trade. Labs were hidden way up in dark hollers and out on the empty acreage of long abandoned farms. It'd take more men than he had, a paramilitary force, to root them all out. He had to face the reality that it was Mad Max out there beyond the county roads. Second shift, he had just two deputies driving the whole county. Most days on first shift, only two were open to take calls, with court appearances and compliance using up the hours of his other men.

Elmo had taken to staying on late most nights, even going out in a cruiser himself. He wondered why he ever wanted this job. Especially days like this, with a mother crying her eyes out on his desk. And this wasn't the first time. And, like all the other times, there wasn't but damn-all he could do about it.

All he could do is sit with her and share a cup of that crappy coffee Diane made in the break room. Beyond sharing his sympathies and promising to do all they could to find her boy, he had nothing for her.

"Look, one thing's for sure, Ms. Loomis," he said, looking into her red-lidded eyes visible over the rim of the coffee mug. "No one's gonna come around your place no more, asking you stupid questions. You don't have the answers they want, and they know that. They do. But see, we just don't know what else to do. You understand?"

She nodded.

"But what I need from you is to promise you'll keep thinking *real* hard. There might be something, some *tiny* little thing you remember, or that your boy said one time, something that may seem like nothing to you now, but that we can maybe use. You do that for me?"

She nodded once again, lowering the mug and offering a shy smile.

"I'm so sorry to bother you like this…" she began.

"Now, this is my job, girl. It's not any kind of bother." And he meant it, though he sensed the tears were about to start flowing again. He quickly stood and rounded the desk to offer her a hand so she could stand. Ushering Carline to the door, he called for Diane to make sure Ms. Loomis made it to her car all right.

Elmo took a seat behind his desk again. His eyes scanned the wall of framed citations and newspaper clippings and pictures of him posing with the governor and the colonel of the State Highway Patrol. It all seemed like so much playacting and dress-up at times like this. All the guns and cars and radios and trappings of police work, and they couldn't find one little boy. His wife would tell him that he was doing the best he could, to think of all the cases he'd closed, and people whose lives he'd saved or improved since he put on the uniform.

Only it was the failures he remembered. They came to mind to wake him up in the morning, or make it hard to drop off at night without a pill or two, and it was worse now than it was when he was out on the roads in his county car. He was the man in charge now, the guy with the answers. It all came to his desk.

"She'll be okay, bless her heart," Diane said, poking her head back in. "Anything else I can do, Sheriff?"

"Get me the district attorney on the line again," he said. "I'm gonna light a fire under his ass."

"Yes, sir," Diane said, moving to close the door.

"And Diane? Send a clerk down to the Circle K to bring me back some *real* coffee."

After the usual exchange about families and some mutual ball-busting about the approaching football season, Elmo got to the nub with the county DA.

"Am I gonna get that help you promised on this, Stan?" The sheriff took a long pull of gas station coffee.

"I gave my word," the district attorney said. "Got a state AAG coming in and getting up to speed on it on Monday."

"Jesus, man. That's the whole weekend shot."

"You're not the only one stretched thin. As it is, he'll be doubling up on this for me."

"You have any other disappearances going in county? Kids, I mean."

"Always got kids going missing. Not an epidemic but it's a constant thing. You know that. Most go off with one parent or the other, some runaways. Sad to say, most turn out to be overdoses."

"I know. Had a kid up here, eleven-year-old, died of the oxy. Eleven."

"Only so much the law can do about that sort of thing," the voice on the phone said.

"No stopping it. Most we can do is slow it down," Elmo said.

"More and more, I think we don't fight wickedness so much as inconvenience it."

"There's that. You maybe have any other kids gone missing up at my end of the county?"

"There's one up near Haley. Another boy 'bout the age of this..." A rustle of papers. "This Cade boy. Same kind of story to yours, good kid, no record. Just vanished off the street on the way home from school."

"In county?"

"Just west of the interstate. The stepdad has some pull. Got the state cops on it right away."

"I should've been told about that, Stan."

"I'll have the ADA pull it all together for you. Might be a connection."

"Some sick son of a bitch pulling boys off the street," Elmo said.

"Well, let's do what we can to inconvenience him. You take it easy now, Elmo." The line went dead.

I'll inconvenience him all the way to Hell, Elmo thought, taking a sip of his coffee. It had gone cold and bitter.

12

"You need to find a job, nephew," Uncle Fern said.

"I had a job," Levon said.

"Daddy's retired," Merry said.

It was Sunday morning, pancake morning as proclaimed by Merry. She was at the stove, ladling batter into an iron skillet. Hope was assisting by slicing bananas.

"Well, your daddy has a lot more money than most retirees," Fern said, turning his chair at the kitchen table to address her. "The taxman will want to know where that money comes from, and 'I found it in a coffee can buried in the yard' ain't gonna wash."

"You think I'm gonna get audited?" Levon said as he poured himself some more coffee.

"Uncle Sam's got a long memory," Fern said. "You think you're clean with those folks? They still have you on their shit list with a star by your name."

"Language," Merry said from the stove. Hope pulled a face, stifling a giggle.

"So, I need a job, you're saying," Levon said.

"Still filing a return, right? How you gonna explain the new trucks out front? The additions to the house. The new garage? Those horses?"

"What kind of a job you think I should apply for?"

"Any kind of job. How should I know?" Fern was getting annoyed. His nephew was playing with him.

"*Any* kind of job is not going to explain away a $60,000.00 garage paid for in cash, and cash for the horses, trucks, fencing, your surgery, new roofs, resurfacing the driveway, that new tractor..."

"All right. All right. I hear you, okay?" Fern said.

"Maybe I should try out for the NFL or see if NASA is hiring."

"You are a ball-buster, nephew." But Fern was smiling over the rim of his bulldog coffee mug.

"Again, language." Hope this time.

"Why don't you start a business?" Merry said as she set down a steaming plate piled with cakes before the men.

"You mean to launder the money," Levon said.

"That's how it's done, right?" Merry said, setting a glass bottle of syrup by her father.

"What do we know about running a business?" Fern said as he lifted a cake to slide a pat of butter under it. "Only business I ever ran was when I was running whiskey."

"Then that's the business we'll open," Levon said.

"You're gonna put 'bootlegger' on your tax return? You been staying up too late on that computer," Fern said. "They lock people away in federal prison for that."

"Not if they're licensed," Levon said.

After a moment's consideration, a grin spread across Fern Cade's face that was a sight to see.

———

"You at home?" Levon said into the phone, the landline on the kitchen wall. Fern was asleep in his easy chair in the family room. The girls were mucking stalls. Levon was alone but for the bluetick pup asleep in a dog bed in a corner near the oven.

"Out on a call." Jessie Hamer's voice.

"On Sunday?"

"Alpacas get sick on Sundays."

"Alpacas?"

"There's an alpaca farm up on Sawyer Road. Some rich bitches from Atlanta playing farmer."

"'Rich bitches'?"

"That's what their vanity plate on their Jag says. Maureen and Janice."

"Sisters?"

"Only in the political sense. They're married."

"What makes an alpaca sick on Sunday?" Levon said.

"Parasites," Jessie said. "I'm halfway through dosing the herd. Sandy's helping."

"How's she feel about that?"

"She thought they were cute until the first one spit on her."

"You gonna be free later?"

"Sure, if you give me time to take a shower and change clothes. They spit on me too. What's the plan?"

"I want to go talk to that friend of Trevor's over to Tall Pines."

"And, you thought having a woman along would look more proper."

"That's the idea."

"I'll call you when I get back home," she said.

"Bye," he said

==

13

Tall Pines had been home to the Black population of Haley since Reconstruction. The neatly laid out grid of streets stretched west of what was once the main train line, now a paved bike trail. The area was more of a mix these days, attracted by the lower rents.

The houses were shotgun shacks for the most part, with a few garden apartment buildings built back in the '50s that were now assigned as Section Eight housing. There was a strip mall that had seen better days anchored by a shuttered ACE Hardware, a barbershop, salon, check cashing place, and a thrift shop. A converted Hardee's sat on the lot. It was now the locally owned John John's Chicken.

There were more churches than bars, mostly wood-frame structures with grass lawns for parking. The biggest church, a brick-faced structure with a three-story steeple, was home to the Southern Baptist congregation. The Methodists had a breeze block building roofed in brass on an asphalt lot. Church of Christ was in a double-wide set back in some woods. Farther back in those same woods was a shot house that Levon knew from his time running whiskey for his uncle, two trips a week to that place with a trunk full of white.

The home of Delbert Washington sat on a willow-lined boulevard with a neatly mowed median strip down the center. Larger homes that once belonged to the neighborhood's dentists, doctors, and lawyers lined either side of this street. Once these houses were show-places. Now they were broken up into apartments; many had outside staircases added decades before.

The Washington apartment was two doors down from the Strode Funeral Home, the oldest family busi-ness in Tall Pines. Levon pulled his truck to a stop in the driveway that ran alongside the house back to what was once a carriage house and now a two-car garage. He and Jessie got out of the cab.

"Does this count as a date?" Jessie said as they climbed the steps to the front porch.

"If you want it to," he said. "I'll take you to dinner when we're done here."

"I'll take it. It'll be like we're a real couple."

"We *are* a real couple, Jess." He pressed the buzzer next to a paper slip with *The Washingtons* neatly hand-printed on it in marker.

"Why, sir, that sounds like a commitment."

Their exchange was interrupted by a little girl in cornrows who opened the door just enough to allow her to give the white folks on the porch a studied gaze.

"We're looking for Delbert," Levon said.

"Mom! Somebody's for Del!" the little girl said, turning her head to call back into the house.

A petite Black woman in her thirties came to the door and opened it wide. She was wiping her hands on her apron. A dusting of flour across the bridge of her nose. She was smiling but her eyes were cautious. The little girl stood just behind, peeping around her mother's leg at the strangers.

"You're looking for my boy?"

Levon explained the reason for his visit and why he wanted to speak to her son. He introduced Jessie as—he cleared his throat—a friend. Jessie's smile went a bit crooked, enjoying Levon's discomfort.

The woman introduced herself as Alondra Washington and welcomed them into her home; an apartment that shared the first floor of the big house with another. She sent Trisha, the little girl, to fetch her big brother from a back room. They stood in a foyer room shared by the first-floor occupants. There was an impressive stained-glass window still intact over the double front doors. A potted fern sat on a marble topped buffet table that was probably a legacy from the house's original owners. The black and white tile floor was clean and waxed but showing its age.

"It's a terrible thing. Trevor is such a nice boy, a quiet boy."

"We only have a few questions, maybe something he might have remembered."

"Could be, Mr. Cade," Alondra said. "The police came by and barely talked to him."

"Please call me Levon."

"Hope you don't mind sitting in the kitchen," she said as she turned and led them to the back of the house. "I got pie crust going and you can't let it sit."

"The kitchen will be fine. Thank you," Jessie said.

Alondra insisted on making them some coffee. She set mugs and a carton of milk on the table. She poured from a steaming carafe, the rich scent of hazelnut filling the room.

Del Washington entered the kitchen with eyes moving from his mother to the strangers.

"This man's a cousin of Trevor's," Alondra said. "He wants to ask you some questions about that day."

"All's I know is what I told the police," Del said, taking a seat in the chair his mother guided him to. Alondra turned back to a wooden cutting board on the counter by the sink where she was trimming circles from a layer of rolled dough.

"Maybe you remember something since then," Levon said. "Something maybe you didn't think was important enough for the deputies."

"Are you a deputy?" the boy said.

"No. I'm just looking out for family. Doing a favor, you know?"

"Uh huh. Yes, sir. Like I told the policemen, Trevor didn't get on the school bus. He told me he had a ride."

"A ride home? Was it with someone you knew?"

"Naw, sir. He told me his dad was coming for him. They were going somewhere together."

"He told you his father was picking him up at school? Had that ever happened before?"

"No, sir. I never met his dad, his *real* dad."

"He didn't mean his stepdad?"

"No, sir. I met his stepdad a bunch of times. He never called his stepdad 'dad.' Only ever called him Victor. Said he liked calling him that 'cause it made his stepdad mad, only his stepdad couldn't say anything or it'd start a fight with his mom."

"And you never met Trevor's father? You know what he looks like?"

"No, sir. I never met him. Trevor says he was away a lot. He only saw him on weekends sometimes."

"You told the deputies about that?"

"They were state police," Alondra said from where she worked at the counter. "They weren't with the sheriff."

Levon considered that. Jessie spoke to the boy to fill the silence.

"Uniformed troopers?" he asked.

The boy nodded.

"You and Trevor are best friends?" Jessie said, taking care to use present tense.

"Yes, ma'am. We do almost everything together."

"They've had sleepovers. Here and at Rowena's," his mother said. "They both love playing their games."

"Is there anything else you remember about that day?" Levon said.

"No, sir."

"How was Trevor acting?"

"We only had the one class together that day and ate lunch with each other," Del said. "But he was happy. Real happy that him and his dad were gonna spend a few days together."

Jessie turned to look at Levon. He said nothing, eyes fixed somewhere in space. The knuckles of the hand that gripped the coffee mug had paled to white.

14

"I don't have the slightest idea what you're talking about, Levon," Rowena said. They were at the kitchen table now in the house on Cherokee Court. There was no smell of homemade pies baking and no offer of coffee. The counters and island were free of any food preparation of any kind. This was a showplace, not a workspace.

"The Washington boy says Trevor was spending the weekend with his father. You say you didn't know that?" Levon said. He was there alone. He'd dropped Jessie off at home before heading back to Haley.

"She told you already," Victor Abruzzi said from where he was leaning back on the sink counter, something amber on ice in a glass in his fist. Vic wore a Tire Kingdom tee-shirt, tight over gym muscle and a salon tan. Rings gleamed on his fingers.

The two girls, older than Trevor by a few years, were in an adjoining family room watching television. It was a show with a live audience whose oohs and aahs in unison sounded like ocean waves.

"It wasn't his weekend. Hell, he missed most of the weekends that *were* his weekends," Rowena said.

"You think he'd want to see his kids, all the time he missed by being in jail," Victor added.

"Did you think of asking Teddy Lee these questions?" Rowena said.

"I can't get ahold of him. The number he gave me is no good," Levon said.

"You try his house?" Victor said. The bitterness was plain in his voice.

"The address he gave me up here is some woman he was seeing. She says she hasn't seen him in weeks."

Rowena made a *pssht* sound with her lips. "Typical."

"Don't you think you should be asking that fuck-up these questions?" Victor said, pushing himself off the counter.

"I think I'm gonna have to do that," Levon said, standing up to look down at the smaller man who was a good head shorter than him.

"Where you gonna look then?" Rowena said. There was a glimmer of amusement on her face at her new husband preening and flexing in the presence of another alpha male in his barnyard. Levon was looking right through him, thoughts a million miles away.

"I know some of the places he hangs out. Someone's seen him."

"I know some of those places too," Rowena said with a knowing smile. "Better watch your ass, Levon."

———

On the way back to Colby, Levon stopped in at a Carrabba's off the interstate and picked up three orders of the seafood and a pasta dish Jessie liked. While he waited on the order, he crossed the lot to the ABC and picked up a bottle of Marsala that was her favorite.

"I should be mad at you," Jessie said when she answered the door.

"*I'm* not mad at you!" Sandy proclaimed as she relieved him of the bags of takeout. "Did you get that olive oil dip stuff?"

"It's in the bag," Levon said, pulling the paper bag wrapped bottle from his jacket pocket.

"This is a cooking wine, you idiot," she said. But Jessie was smiling as she slipped an arm around his waist.

"You told me you liked it."

"Yeah, when I'm roasting a chicken." She guided him toward the kitchen where Sandy was pulling covered takeout containers of salads and entrées from the bags.

"Mom said you're trying to find your cousin," Sandy said as they ate at the table in the breakfast nook off the kitchen.

"Not having much luck at it either," Levon said. He filled them in on what he'd learned at the Abruzzi house.

"Your old girlfriend didn't have anything useful to add?" Jessie said, eyes glittering. Levon ignored her.

"Rowena didn't know anything about Teddy taking the boy that weekend. It wasn't something they talked about."

"Maybe Teddy took his son. That's usually what happens in cases like this. It's a parent," Jessie said.

"It's always the parent on the TV shows," Sandy said around a mouthful of oil-dipped bread.

"Then why would Teddy ask me to look for him?" Levon said. "Doesn't make sense."

"I hate to say that the bitch is right, but you need to see what your cousin has to say," Jessie said. "Somebody's lying here."

Levon nodded. Jessie was right. Someone was lying. He strongly suspected that everyone was lying.

15

Dreams and waking blended into one in the room with the flowery walls. He had displeased Dads and so remained locked in the room with nothing to do but sleep and watch the shadows move across the cracked plaster of the sky-blue ceiling.

Russ wanted nothing more than to be free of this room. It was a cage. He knew that. It was a place where he was held like a dog in a kennel, and he *was* the dog, a bad dog. Dads promised that he would be released from the room, be allowed to go downstairs and play games and eat ice cream with the other boys. Only Russ could not make himself do what Dads wanted him to do. No matter how many of the pills he swallowed, he could not do as he was told.

Dads brought another man to see him, a man who smelled sour with beer and cigarettes. A white man with dark arms and the fish belly pallor on his chest and belly that Russ's mama called a farmer's tan. He was told to be good to the man, to be nice to the man. The man had a game he liked to play and if Russ played it with him there would be a reward afterward, but the man wanted to hurt Russ, hurt him a different way than Dads had with the toys. Russ screamed and scratched and kicked, forced face down on the bed, bucking like a landed trout till Dads came in the room roaring. The two men had a fight then, bad words and shoving until the man left, calling Dads all kinds of filthy names.

Once the man was gone, Dads took a loop of knotted clothesline to Russ. He stropped Russ across the back and rump until Russ surrendered to the pain, passing out on the floor by the bed.

It was a whole day before he woke up again. He was on the bed in clean pajamas. Some kind of greasy salve that smelled like mint had been smeared on his back and butt. A sandwich and a glass of milk gone warm sat atop the dresser on a dish towel. He wasn't hungry but he ate it anyway, ham and cheese with bread gone stale and the cheese pasty.

Russ had to pee and there was nowhere to do so in the little room. The idea of knocking at the door was unthinkable. The stabbing pain in his bladder sharpened. He had to pee. He thought of the empty milk glass but was afraid it would not hold all he had to release. Peeing on the floor would only bring more punishment, bad dog again. He went to the window and parted the heavy drapes. He unlocked the latch atop the lower casement. It took all his strength, as it had been painted shut. With his fingers in two depressions set the bottom of the wooden frame, he pulled upward. There was a crackling sound and then the window was free, sliding upward to create a gap of eight inches or more. The air outside was cooler, cleaner.

On his tiptoes, Russ pulled down the front of his

pajama bottoms and let it flow out over the sill under the iron bars and onto the surface of a lower roof. He gasped with the sudden relief of it. When he was finished, he lowered the sash until only a two-inch gap remained. He drew the drapes closed once more and returned to the bed.

The simple exertion of opening the window left him weak. His head felt light, the floor beneath him shifting, the walls yawing back and forth like a ship at sea. Russ fought to keep the sandwich and milk down, turning on his side atop the covers until the vertigo passed from him.

He lay like that a long while, afraid to move even the slightest bit in fear that the dizziness might come back. The muscles in his legs became stiff and he shifted to relieve the discomfort. It didn't go away. His joints hurt. His jaw and neck as well. His eyes felt hot. His skin felt dry and tight as though it were contracting, shrinking onto his bones.

Russ turned to lay on his back and will himself toward the comfort of sleep. It did not come.

He focused his gaze on the ceiling, on the solitary crack that ran across the plastered surface. He imagined that the jagged crack was a river that divided two lands, two kingdoms. The pale blue surface became a snow-covered land at dusk. He imagined a frozen steppe and two peoples struggling to survive on either side of the river. His eyes lost focus entirely as he surrendered to a waking dream of medieval warfare and fantasy warriors and mythical creatures. He sank deeper into the trance he created until it seemed more real than the little room and the angry men and the pain he felt across his entire body.

A massive castle rose from the frigid wastes, and before it a besieging army of men and beasts striking at the walls with rams and missiles from catapults. Staunch defenders sent clouds of arrows from the tops of the walls that felled mountains of dead that the savage invaders crawled over to near the walls of the mighty stronghold.

Massed troops of men and near-men crowded the span of a broad drawbridge to force the iron head of a massive ram against the brass-bound gate of the walled city. The ram pounded the metal surface again and again and again. The thunder of it rising even over the shrieks of the dying as arrows and bolts fell in a deadly hail from the towers and ramparts above.

Boom.

Boom.

Boom.

Russ blinked. The deep vision vanished and all he saw was the ceiling above, divided in an X formed by the diagonal crack and the narrow bar of reflected light from the pole lamp coming through the gap in the drapes.

The frozen world of two armies locked in mortal struggle was gone but the rhythmic sound of the ram remained. It wasn't a resonant thud but a tapping.

Three taps.

He listened hard; his breath held.

Three more taps. They came from the wall above him, a wall shared with the room next to his.

Russ rose to stand on the bed, his ear held pressed to the wallpaper. Three more taps just inches from his ear, sounding sharper now. He answered with his own tap using the knuckles of his fisted hand on the wallpaper. He pressed his ear tight to the wall.

Four taps.

He climbed down the bed to pick up the empty milk glass. Returning to his place atop the mattress, he tapped the base of the glass against the wall four times.

Five taps.

He answered with five taps of his own.

The reply was three taps in close succession. The source had moved. It was lower on the wall now. He crouched on the bed to tap a reply, three more taps even lower on the wall. He answered. The next set of taps came from a place under the bed.

Russ dropped to the floor and slid on his belly into the shadows beneath the bed. The taps came again, and he pulled himself across the wooden floor toward the sound. He could see a glow there, a pinpoint of illumination just above the top of the baseboard.

He lay on his side, adjusting his vision to a tiny hole, no wider than a finger, in the wallpaper. It was ripped there, the corners of the rip protruding, forced outward by whoever had created the hole from the other side. With his fingers he peeled the corners of the ripped wallpaper aside to reveal a ragged hole in the plaster, crumbs of ancient gypsum and horsehair batting falling away as he dug his end of the hole wider with his fingertip.

With a foot braced against the base of one of the bed's posts, he pressed an eye to the hole.

A single blue eye with pale blond lashes stared at him from the other side of the wall.

16

"You girls got everything you need?" Levon said as he pulled the Avalanche onto the lot of Edmund Pettis Middle School. He joined a line of minivans and SUVs dropping off other kids.

"Yes, Dad," Merry and Hope said in unison from the back seat. They clutched their book bags, looking eager, faces shiny and bright. New jeans, sneakers, and tops.

"And you'll look out for one another?"

"Yes, Dad."

"And you'll wait right here for your Uncle Fern?"

"Come on, Dad," Merry said.

"Where will you be today?" Hope asked.

"I have a few places I have to go. Not sure I'll be back in time for you."

"You seeing Jessie?" Merry said. He could see the pair of them in the rearview sharing a look with repressed smiles.

"No. She's got work to do. I'm doing Cousin Teddy a favor."

"About his son?" Merry said.

"Yeah. I have a few more questions I need to ask people. Tried calling Teddy, but his phone's no good."

"Happy hunting," Merry said.

"Okay then," he said as the truck arrived at the drop-off zone. A smiling older woman wearing a yellow sash that read VOLUNTEER GRANDMOM opened the rear passenger door.

"Hello, girls. You know your homeroom assignments?"

"Yes, ma'am," both girls said as they dropped from the truck.

"'Ma'am.' I *like* that," the grandmom said and leaned in to speak to Levon before shutting the door. "Good job, Dad!"

The Mount Epson Trailer Estate had seen better days. It sprawled out along winding gravel lanes lined with loblolly pines. Most of the trailers showed signs of neglect—rust along the edges, broken lattice skirts around their bases, or no skirts at all. A number of roofs were repaired with blue tarps held in place with nylon cordage. As sad as the dwellings were, the vehicles were an impressive array of hillbilly war machines. These folks had their priorities, and they went beyond the pride of home ownership, jacked-up trucks, Harleys, and ATVs in every variation of camouflage. In addition, there were bass boats on trailers and even a few jet skis up on cinder blocks. Each bang-up had a satellite dish secured either on the roof or set up atop a creosote pole.

A lot of the trailers had "For Sale by Owner" signs set in the postage stamp of grass that passed for a yard. Even sadder, a few were advertised for rent.

"I'll tell you what I told his PO, and what I already told you before," Nadine Welles said around the stub of a Marlboro, holding the screen door of her single-wide open. "I ain't seen Teddy Lee around here in weeks, nor do I wish to."

Teddy was ducking his parole officer. That told Levon something. His cousin was in some kind of serious bind. It was something that offered more of a threat than the law, more than being thrown back into a cell at Bullock.

"What'd he do to get such a long parole term?"

"Thought you knew him. What's your name, anyway?"

"Levon Cade, just like Teddy."

"Shit. He talked about you. You some kind of war hero or like that?"

"What'd he do to need to be on probation this long?"

"Lost his shit when they busted him, all fucked up on rock. Busted a trooper's jaw with a wrench. They take that shit personal."

"You don't know where he'd be now?"

"Not only don't I know, I see no reason why I'd tell you to start with."

"Shame. I had some money for him," Levon said, his voice raised to be heard over the insistent barking of a pit bull straining at a chain on the next lot.

"You did?" Nadine brightened. "You could let me hold it for him. I'll make sure he gets it."

"No, I think it's best I hand it to him personally."

Nadine made a pout before lighting a fresh cigarette from the butt of the last one.

"I can't help you. Like I said, he ain't been sniffin' around here of late."

"He ever have a kid with him when he visited? A little boy?"

"You mean his son? He talked about him sometimes. Never brought him 'round."

"Maybe you know where Teddy might be now?" Levon held a twenty up between his fingers.

"What's that for?" Nadine's nose wrinkled.

"A finder's fee."

"You double that, and I might just invite you inside." Nadine leered through a wreath of blue smoke.

"Wish I had time, honey, but I really need to see Teddy."

"You know the Locust, the roadhouse near Stillwater? And he was seeing a bitch works down at the Hampton Inn. A friend of mine works there told me that. That's when I threw him out."

"I know the Locust."

"Then there's Plank's. He liked going there some nights. Might find him there, maybe."

"I remember that place. Back up the mill road?"

"Yeah. Real shithole, just right for a pig like Teddy." Nadine plucked the twenty from Levon's fingers and gave him a look of fresh appraisal. "What do you owe him money for? You don't look much like one of his friends."

"We're cousins."

She barked at that.

"Can't pick our relations, can we?"

———

Plank's BBQ was nothing more than a shack at the end of a crushed stone road that followed Crumb's Run, a creek that went from a trickle in summer to an engorged swell with snowmelt come spring. The building started life as a saw shed until the new mill was built farther north when the county got hooked to the electric grid.

Since then, the place had become a watering hole for shine runners, supplanted by meth cookers and tourists looking for a taste of danger. Thanks to an article in *Garden and Gun* magazine, Plank's had a new reputation as a weekend destination for adventurous motorcycle riders up from Huntsville and down from Chattanooga. The rusted metal roof was painted a bright yellow and pennants and Chinese lanterns hung from lines strung over the rows of picnic tables. Nothing else had changed. There was still the burnt black barrel of a massive barbeque smoker and rows of standing coolers behind a long wooden bar topped with galvanized aluminum.

A heavy-set Black man stood over racks of ribs, daubing them with a house painting brush he dipped in a plastic tub of thick red goop. He wore a once-white apron and his head was wrapped in a bandanna with "Man of God" printed across his brow. A single waitress, a leggy brunette in denim cutoffs, cowboy boots and a tight white Plank's T-shirt, was bringing orders to the only two occupied tables. Four pickups sat under the trees along the lane. Come the weekend, there'd be motorcycles here by the dozens, the tables packed with part-time badasses in the leathers they traded for their weekday business suits.

Levon stepped into the shade to the bar. A sleepy-looking good old boy lifted his ass off a stool to take his order.

"Just a Coke," Levon said.

"You want that fortified with anything?" the man said with a drawl that told the world he was in no hurry to get anywhere and had all day to do it in.

"Just the pop."

The man fished an ice-cold glass bottle from a tub under the counter and popped the top before placing it atop a paper coaster.

"It's that Mexican Coke," he said as Levon took a pull. "Only thing they make better than us."

"I'm guessing they made *them*." Levon nodded to the trucks parked in the shade of the trees.

"You prolly right 'bout that. Getting's so even American things ain't American no more." The man shrugged and turned to his stool.

"I'm looking for my cousin. I heard he comes around here now and then." Levon set a fresh twenty on the counter and placed the bottle atop it.

"Might be if he's a local boy. Best pulled pork anywhere." The man took a renewed interest in their conversation while setting another Coke on the bar.

"He goes by Lee or Teddy Lee. Drives a piece-of-shit 150 with a lift kit. Bit of family resemblance, but he's all inked up and heavier than me."

"Shit, boy, ain't hardly no one don't have a family resemblance back up in here."

"Well, I hear he comes here. He'd be a regular."

"I might have seen him. I could ask around for you, if you like."

"I'd appreciate that," Levon said, leaving the empty and the twenty behind.

When he got to his truck, he turned back to see the man behind the bar speaking into a cell phone.

17

Plank's was his last stop of the day. He took his time sipping a second Coke in the cab of his truck under the shade of a big oak.

Levon knew he was stirring the pot by asking questions about Teddy Lee. He'd already been by the Locust, a blood bucket with a shot room in the back. They knew his cousin there and told him Teddy was blacklisted. Levon didn't ask what a man needed to do to violate the rules in a place like that.

The day manager at the Hampton Inn remembered Teddy, too. He caught Teddy and one of the maids, a Honduran girl, naked in the jacuzzi.

"She was on the clock and on his cock," the day manager said with a hoot. "Fired her little brown ass there and then. Haven't seen her since. Him neither."

His cousin was making some kind of local legend of himself. Levon's last option was Plank's. There was one more place Teddy could be, but Levon wanted to avoid looking there if he could. His best hope was that someone would spread the word that he was looking for Teddy; someone who wanted Teddy for themselves.

He didn't have long to wait. They were waiting for him as he gave up on waiting to drive away.

A Dodge Ram, all jacked up on twenty-two-inch gunmetal wheels and fat knobby tires, sat athwart the apron at the end of the creek road out of Plank's. There was no way around it since weed-choked gullies ran either side where it joined the township road.

Two men exited the cab as Levon slipped his truck into park. He sat watching them approach, undoing his seat belt while sliding a hand behind him to ear back the hammer on the Colt 1911 resting at the small of his back.

First was a big man, linebacker size with a spreading gut and the rubber butt of a revolver visible in the waistband of his cargo shorts under an untucked work shirt with the sleeves torn off. The other man was near as big and more fit with mirrored shades under a bushy mullet. He was wearing a too-tight tee and skinny jeans. Both men had biker wallets, a loop of chain swinging off their hips. They each had bad prison tats as well. Obviously either cousins or brothers or asshole buddies who'd bunked up in a cell sometime back.

They both halted their advance when Levon stepped from the cab to meet them halfway.

"Something I can do for you?" Levon said. He didn't bother with a smile.

"You can tell us where your cousin is," the fat one said, a wet wheeze in his voice. Levon could smell the nicotine sweat from twenty feet.

"Well, if I could tell you that, I wouldn't be looking for him."

"Don't you talk to him like that." The Mullet hopped on one cowboy boot, voice reedy. A rabbit snarl revealed jagged, blackened teeth, a tweaker.

"What you want with him?" Tubby said.

"Family business, which means not your business."

Mullet made to snort. It came out more like a whistle through his drug-ravaged sinuses.

"He owes us," Tubby said. "Maybe we take it out of you."

Tubby parted his shirt wider to show more of the stainless wheelgun parked snug against his blubber. Mullet smirked, hopping on the other foot now.

Both men froze, chins turned aside and eyes narrowed at the black automatic that seemed to instantaneously appear in Levon's hands, the black eye of it trained on the unmissable target the fat man offered.

"Guns out. Now. Pointing finger and thumbs only. Hold 'em like you'd hold a snapping turtle's tail," Levon said.

They did as they were told, holding handguns out daintily dangled at arm's length, Tubby's a snub barreled .357 while Mullet favored a Glock.

"That it? Don't lie. I'll know."

They believed him. Both men nodded vigorously.

"Toss 'em clear. Easy lob. Toward me."

The men did as they were told. Tubby's piggy eyes focused on Levon, his face turned ruddy.

"Lie down. On your bellies. Hands behind heads."

Mullet assumed the position with practiced ease. For the other man, it was a monumental task that involved a lot of groans and winces. Levon stepped forward to pick up each gun and toss them far into the broad-leafed undergrowth that ran along the creek bank.

"You, with the hair, you move that truck out of my way. Then you come right back here."

"He's got the keys," Mullet said, head craned up to look at the weapon aimed at him.

"Then get the keys."

Mullet rose to his knees to dig in the bigger man's pockets. He came up with change, bills, a smartphone, and finally a ring of keys. He looked to Levon who nodded.

"You move the truck, but if you got a shotgun in the cab like I bet you do, you remember I have your buddy here. He'll die, then you'll die."

Mullet's head bobbed as he backed toward the Dodge, hands up and the keyring swinging from his fingers.

Levon spoke to the prone man while keeping the .45 and his eyes locked on the other making his way to the Dodge.

"You say Teddy Lee owes you. What's he owe you?"

"Money, you dumb shit. What else you think he'd owe us?"

"How much?"

"Still owes $30 outtaK forty. We give him a break, break's over, and he needs to get even."

"He already paid ten?"

"Yeah. He give us something on account, but it ain't paid till the last dollar's handed over."

"That's good enough," Levon called over the rumbling engine of the truck. "Cut the motor and bring the keys on back here."

Mullet climbed down from the cab and made his way back, jingling the keys before him.

"What's he owe you for?" Levon asked Tubby.

"Protection when he was in Bullock. Some nigger boys wanted his ass, they like that sweet white ass, our outfit provided it. Now he pays up."

"What about the Aryans? Why didn't he go to them instead of your crew?"

"Your cuz was the only Nazi in our section. None of his friends were locked up there."

Mullet had returned. Levon had him toss the keys toward the creek before lying down on the roadway again.

"Where else have you looked for him?" Levon asked.

"We come here first. We heard he likes this place," Mullet offered.

"He ain't here, and don't try his girlfriend, not his ex either. No one's seen him. You stay out of my way and let me find him. I'll make sure he gets right with you plus two thousand."

"What's the extra for?" Tubby said, the wheeze more pronounced from lying on the ground this long.

"Two new tires. I'm gonna shoot 'em flat before I leave."

"Aw, shit no," Mullet hissed.

"We're gonna meet again, son," Tubby said, voice a rumble.

Levon said nothing. He returned to his truck and got into the cab. The pair on the road rose to their feet to step aside as he drove past. The fat man, eyes dark under beetled brows, stared at Levon as he pulled past. Up on the road Levon pulled level with the Dodge and pumped two rounds each into the tires on the passenger side. The big sled sagged like a ship holed on the starboard side.

He drove off, leaving the men to root through the ferns and sumacs for their guns and keyring.

18

Merry and Hope were assigned different lunch periods, so the first time they saw one another was at the end of the day when they joined the crowd of kids boarding school buses or waiting for pick-ups.

They talked over each other. There was so much to share. Merry's favorite subject was history, but her social studies teacher was an indifferent bore. Hope shared her amazement at all the free books and each student having a desk of their own.

A pair of girls Merry had sat with at lunch joined them. Merry introduced her "sister" to Kelly and Sarah and turned from Hope to speak to them. A boy approached Hope to say something in Spanish to her.

Hope turned to the boy, eyes wide. The boy was older than she was, older than most of the other kids here, she thought. He was almost as dark as her, with a wisp of chin hair and his head shaved high at the sides and back. His fingers were stained yellow, and he had a small cross with three stars inexpertly tattooed on the web of his right hand. She noticed he carried no book bag.

"You talk, don't you?" he said to her, still in Spanish.

"Yes, I talk," Hope answered in English.

"Come on, don't pretend to be a *gabacha* with me," he said. He was smiling at her in a way she didn't like.

"I don't know what that means," she said, and she didn't, it being a slur for whites used more commonly in Mexico.

"But you understand what I'm saying to you?" His smile took on a mocking tilt. "What are you? Honduran? Nicaraguan? You're not Dominican, not dark enough."

Hope backed away from the boy, bumping into Merry who turned from her new friends.

"Who's this guy?" Merry asked.

"I don't know," Hope said. "He just started talking to me."

"I was talking to her, not you," the boy said, in English now. His English came easy with only a trace of an accent.

"And now you are talking to me," Merry said in Spanish. "She's my little sister and I don't like her talking to boys we don't know, and I'm sure we don't want to know you."

"Your sister? *Mierda*." He snorted.

Hope tugged at the hem of Merry's blouse and pointed to Uncle Fern's pickup approaching along the line of queuing cars coming off the driveway. Merry took Hope by the hand and brushed past the strange boy for their uncle's truck. The boy said something to Merry under his breath as she passed him. Fern leaned across the bench seat to pop the passenger door for the girls, and they climbed in.

"What did that boy say to you?" Hope asked in Spanish so that Fern would not understand.

"*Nada*," Merry said, her face turned to her window.

Merry's cheeks were red, and her mouth set hard. Hope suspected that whatever the boy said either embarrassed Merry or made her angry, or both.

19

Levon switched the Avalanche to four-wheel drive to make the push up the steep grade of the narrow packed-stone roadway. It climbed the spine of a ridge that stretched out from the peak of Cooper's Rise, a tree-covered hummock of high country with rocky blades of land dropping away to the east from the summit like fingers splayed from a hand. The ridges created deep valleys between them, making nameless hollers created by nature for hiding stills, bodies, and secrets.

Ferns and scrub slapped and scraped at the truck's fenders where they overhung the passageway. The truck bucked and dipped violently where the wheels dropped into ruts created by runoff. He gunned it hard, taking the jolts that slammed him against the steering wheel and once knocked his head against the ceiling. Slowing down here meant getting stuck and a long walk down to the roadway. The heartbreak hill led to a hunting camp he'd seen a time or two when off-season hunting up this way as a kid.

The roadway broadened a bit as the incline became

gentler and finally leveled out onto a clearing in the trees where a sagging old cabin sat on a shelf below the peak, a wood frame structure abandoned by whoever built it decades before. It was overgrown now with maple saplings and juniper brush. Levon remembered it from the days of his youth when the ground around it was kept clear and spread with cedar chips. There was a big stack stone barbecue pit in front of the cabin. It was collapsed now in a shapeless heap of stones.

He and his brother Dale used that barbecue a time or two when they'd camped up here on overnight hunts. They'd slept in the bunks in the cabin too, breaking the hasp on the padlock to gain entry. It was always off-season, months before the owners would be coming up the hill looking for whitetail. Still, it was an adventure, as if they were escaped convicts or outlaws on the run. The boys awakened at noises in the middle of the night thinking it might be the cabin's owner coming up the gravel road. The fear of discovery was part of the fun.

Levon parked the Avalanche and climbed from the cab to slip on a canvas farmer's coat. It was cooler up here near the hilltop. He opened the rear door of the crew cab and dropped the seat back forward. There was a padded rifle case concealed in the space behind the seat. From this he withdrew a Ruger Mini-14 with a black Rynex stock. He slipped a pair of charged magazines from a side pouch on the case and slid those into a pocket of the coat. A third magazine, he secured in place on the rifle and worked the action to chamber a round.

The rifle slung over his shoulder, he hiked south away from the cabin to follow a trail down into the next holler over. The trees grew denser as he descended, and soon the ceiling of the forest blotted out the afternoon sky to create a gray twilight.

He had a general idea of where he was heading. Though he'd hunted and hiked this country many times before, he'd never been to the floor of this valley. The threat of an angry owner turning up unexpectedly to find two boys squatting in his cabin was harmless fun, but the stories about the holler he was climbing down into were more real than legend. No campfire ghost stories about this place, only history. This was not a place to be visited on a dare.

The trail hooked left and right through the trees to reduce the steep decline down the breakneck slope. Deer tracks were everywhere in the damp earth. Raccoons chittered from somewhere in the trees above him. Squirrels leaped from bough to bough, curious about the solitary man following the switchback, spying on him from where they clung to the thick boles of longleaf pines with one eye exposed to watch.

The hillside dropped down to end at a narrow stream, little more than a runoff fed by a spring farther up in a crotch formed where two ridges, the walls of the holler, joined. Levon followed the flow of the stream until he could see sunlight once more through the trees along the south bank. Crouching, he moved to the edge of the tree line.

A broad clearing lay beyond the trees, running all the way to where the next ridge rose to climb to the top of Cooper's Rise. Hammocked between these fingers of land was a holler called Sugar Run, named for the stream he'd followed down. Here, deep in the forested depression was an oasis of goat grass and foxtail growing nearly as tall as he was. Visible above the silky tips of the grass blades were rusted tin rooftops nestled near a copse of old growth maples. Atop a leaning aluminum tower sat the bent spokes of an actual, ancient, by God, TV antenna.

He crouched, eyes closed, listening rather than looking. There were no sounds other than the natural sounds of the woods on a late summer afternoon, crickets and songbirds, the whisper of the grass.

With the rifle combat slung and held before him, he moved low through the grass until he came near a patch where it had been mown recently, but not too recently. The green stalks were calf height. The mown section was in a rectangle. Toward the maples were wooden benches under a metal-roofed portico that shaded it. In the other direction, fifty yards and then a hundred yards along, were rows of wooden posts driven into the ground. From a few of these hung the yellowed and tattered remains of paper targets, man targets. One was clearly a cartoonish caricature of a black male with exaggerated lips and an afro.

Using the grass as cover, Levon moved east to follow the edge of the shooting range for the collection of buildings under the trees. He reached a long wall of stacked firewood, split and drying and piled in neat cords. Some of it had gone black with rot near the ground causing the stacks to lean at a precarious angle. From here, looking between the cords, he was concealed but had a clear view of the compound.

The main building was an asbestos-sided double-wide with a metal roof streaked orange with rust. There was a prefab outhouse with three doors set up on a wooden deck. It was roofed with a sheet of translucent fiberglass to allow in natural light.

There was a dog run too; a cyclone-fenced surround set on a concrete slab and roofed over with tin sheeting. There were no dogs inside and no evidence any had been there in a long while. The doors to the pens lay open.

Set closest to Levon's hiding place was an open-walled shelter supported by I-beams that looked like the kind of enclosures public parks have for picnickers. There were even rows of wooden picnic tables on the poured concrete slab that formed the floor. The only difference between this structure and a place a family might spend a Memorial Day was the ten-foot flag hanging from the rafters at one end, a red flag with a black swastika in the center of a white oval.

Sugar Run had a reputation going way back. It was the place parents used to scare their kids when nothing else worked. "You behave now, or I'll drop you up Sugar Run and leave you there." It was a place no one unin-vited ever came back. At the height of the Klan's influ-ence, back in his great-granddaddy's time, Levon heard stories about how the smoke from the burning crosses could be seen for miles around. The flames reflected against the clouds turned the overcast into a shim-mering field of orange and umber. Stories were told of lynchings and whippings and rows of graves dug in the red clay, secrets few men knew, even fewer now as the Klan's numbers had dwindled and their influence in the county shrank to insignificance.

Levon recalled hearing his father and Uncle Fern speak of Sugar Run sometimes when they'd sit out on the back porch splitting a sixer or a jar of white. And, as poor a role model as his daddy was, Levon recalled his father's oft-repeated summation of the Empire and all its wizards and kleagles and dragons.

"The Klan? They's nothin' but a bunch of assholes," the senior Cade had said on more than one occasion.

Levon kept the picnic enclosure between him and the main building to move in closer. There were two vehicles parked on the packed earth lot in front of the double-wide, a Toyota 4Runner and Teddy Lee's beat-to-shit Ford pickup.

Teddy Lee's head felt like something had crawled inside to hibernate and was just now waking up. He sat at one of the long tables in the open room that served as a meeting hall. He washed down some aspirins with a long pull of coffee.

"Christ on a pony, Albert," he growled in a thick voice. "What the fuck you put in this coffee?"

"That's cowboy coffee, brother," called Albert from the kitchenette off the main room of the double-wide where he was frying some eggs, onions, and sausages.

"Who made it for 'em? The Indians?" Teddy said, taking another sip and pulling a sour face.

"You want that *pussy* coffee, you head on over to Haley to that Starbuckers and shit," Albert called.

Teddy ripped open six sugar packets and dumped them into the mug. All it did was make the mess thicker. He'd choked down half the brew by the time Albert reached the table with two plates of breakfast and a stack of toast balanced on his arms. Albert was tall and rail thin; a tank top hung from his narrow shoulders.

His wiry arms were nearly black with tats from his bony shoulders down his wrists. Daggers, eagles, skulls, and crosses fought for attention on his ropy muscles. Most prominent was a Maltese cross covering most of the right side of his neck above the collar line.

The eggs and slivered onions slid about on the plate atop a lake of grease as Albert set them down on the tabletop. Teddy's stomach clenched in the peculiar mix of nausea and hunger that only a really good hangover can bring on. He absently tore a corner off a piece of toast to sop up at least some of the drippings.

"Bad as this coffee is, that shit last night was worse," Teddy said as he stabbed at a yolk. "My head's banging worsen' your old lady."

"Nothin' wrong with that whiskey last night. That's from my uncle's. That pure sunshine, brother."

"Your uncle gave you piss water off the first run. We're lucky we didn't wake up this mornin' blind."

"You turned pussy on me, Teddy. First bitchin' about the coffee then…" Albert's voice trailed away.

Teddy looked up to see what had caused the hitch in Albert's conversation. He turned on his chair to follow the other man's astonished gaze back toward the open door of the double-wide.

His cousin Levon was in the doorway, a rifle trained on them both.

"Levon?" Teddy said. He blinked his eyes hard, thinking his cousin was a further product of his hangover.

Levon's attention was on his friend.

"That you, Albert Wise?" Levon said, stepping closer. The rifle stayed raised and aimed at the pair of seated men.

"Didn't know you at first, Levon." Albert's voice was level.

"I know you don't go anywhere without a blade, Albert. I need you to show me that blade. Do it real slow and let me see both your hands at once."

Teddy made to speak but his cousin's eyes cut toward him, all the while keeping the Ruger's sights set on Albert.

"You too, Teddy. Put your hands flat on the table."

Both men complied. Albert withdrew a five-inch clasp knife from the back pocket of his jeans as he might hold a dead rat by the tail and tossed it far into a corner of the room.

"You see that Heinz bottle in front of you, Teddy?"

Teddy nodded, looking at the heavy glass ketchup bottle by his plate.

"I want you to take it by the neck and give your friend here a good, solid smack across the head with it."

Albert began to voice an objection.

"You mean that?" Teddy said.

"Make it count, cousin," Levon said. "You don't want to have to do it twice."

"But I might kill him."

"Not if you do it right. It's up to you, Teddy. You coldcock him now or let him listen to what we're about to talk about, and I think you know what I came here to talk about."

Without hesitation, Teddy half stood to take up the twelve-ounce bottle and bring it down hard on the crown of his friend's head. Albert dropped limp from his chair but not before striking his forehead on the edge of the table with an impact like a gunshot.

Levon moved around behind Teddy to bring himself

closer to the fallen man. He planted the steel toe of a work boot in Albert's crotch and applied weight. The man didn't stir. Levon used a toe to turn Albert on his side. All the while, the Ruger stayed trained on his cousin.

"He's gonna want to know why I did that. He's gonna ask what we talked about."

"That's not how head trauma works. He's not gonna remember waking up this morning."

"What you want from me, Levon, you come sneakin' up here like this?"

"Tell me about your time up in Bullock," Levon said.

The sweet acidic sludge of Albert's cowboy brew tried to climb up Teddy's throat in a rush. He fought it down and gasped, eyes tearing and nose running.

"Who you been talkin' to?" His voice small now.

"Some tub of goo and his mullet head friend say you owe them $30,000.00 for keeping your cornhole untroubled up at State."

"Price and Yales. You run into them, huh?"

"I did. I told them I'd make you whole again once I'd talked to you."

"Okay. So, we talked." Teddy snorted and spat, building up his confidence again.

"No. We're *talking* but we ain't talked."

Teddy swallowed hard.

"A few things got me to thinking," Levon said. "You ask me to look for your boy then you vanish on me."

"I got in Dutch with my PO. She was gonna violate me. Couldn't stay around anywhere she might know."

"That doesn't explain why you'd cut me off. You could've let me know where you were. Suppose I found

Trevor. I'd have no way of letting you know. Aren't you worried about him?"

"Shit, yeah, I'm worried!" Teddy said. His voice cracked.

Levon said nothing.

"Can't all be like you," Teddy said, a catch in his throat. "Can't all get our shit together way you did."

"Is that what I did?"

"Fuck, yeah. Got outta here. Joined the army and shit. Moved down to Huntsville in some suburb house."

"All I did was make choices and stick with 'em, Teddy. There's nothing special about me."

"Then you're just a lucky sumbitch, I guess." Teddy sniffed, hawked and spat.

"That tub of goo said you gave them something on account. Something worth ten thousand off what you owe them. I couldn't stop thinking about how he said that. 'Something on account.' That means something worth ten thousand but not ten thousand in cash."

"Why didn't you ask them?"

"'Cause I'm asking you, Teddy."

Teddy stared at him, locked eyes on Levon's over the barrel of the rifle. There was a corona of white around his pupils as he fought not to break from the other man's gaze. His lips were pressed tight, the flesh at the corners of his mouth blanched white. It was then that Levon knew the truth.

"You gave them Trevor," Levon said.

Teddy let out an animal howl and launched himself from his chair. Levon spun the Ruger to drive the butt hard into his cousin's chest. Teddy went down on the floor, wheezing for breath. Levon stood over him, the end of the rifle barrel inches from his face.

"You gave up your son to buy yourself some time," Levon said in a voice barely above a whisper. "You think about what that means? You think about what you sent him into?"

"That's *all* I can think about," Teddy said at last between sobs. His voice sounded like a child's.

Levon stood, the rifle aimed at his cousin's head. The man on the floor could not look at him now. Teddy was turned away, his face wet with tears, his hands clutched like claws before him.

"You sent me after him thinking I'd get him back. You know me. You know I'd not leave anyone behind to draw a line between you and me, and if I got killed, who'd give a damn, it was worth a try."

Teddy mewled. Wordless utterings through bubbling lips.

"I'm weighing now what I'd regret more."

Teddy glanced up at him through swollen lids.

"Whether I'd regret killing you more than leaving you alive."

21

The boy on the other side of the wall was named Jason.

All Russ could see was the blue eye looking back at him through the hole poked in the wall just above the baseboard. Jason sounded younger than he was, his voice higher and softer and with a trace of a lisp.

They spent hours talking to one another that first night. Russ lay on the cold floor, wrapped in a blanket he pulled down from the bed. They spoke in whispers, pausing only when house noises caused them to hush and wait until the silence was restored.

Russ learned that Jason had been here in this house since last summer. He was allowed out of his room only to take a bath now and then. He was fed in his room and given a bucket to pee and dump in.

"They never let you downstairs?" Russ asked.

"One time. It was Christmas, I think. Near to, maybe? Charlie Brown was on the TV."

"Why do some boys get to be downstairs?"

"They're the good boys, maybe? You do what Dads says. You don't sass back. You get to be downstairs."

"You're not a good boy?"

"Tried to hurt myself, while back. Dads was so mad. Brought someone to the house for me. A doctor. Look."

The eye shifted from the hole. Russ looked through to see a shadow cross the circle of light. He blinked and focused, not sure what he was looking at, a jagged line of puckered white flesh, a scar healed on a hairless forearm pink as a puppy's belly. Russ felt an icy ball form in his stomach.

"You did that to yourself?" Russ said when the blue eye had returned.

"Didn't want to be here. Thought if I wasn't here no more, no one could hurt me."

"You shouldn't do that. You shouldn't hurt yourself."

"Don't want to do what I'm told. Don't care about going downstairs or getting ice cream. I just want to leave. Any way I can."

The boy went quiet. Russ waited, his ear turned to the hole. It was a long time before the whispered voice through the wall resumed.

"Any way I can." The voice was frailer now and far away.

He could only see gray emptiness through the hole. Russ rapped on the plaster with his knuckles until the eye returned.

"You can't leave like that. Someone will find us. Someone is looking for us."

"No. No one can ever find us. Dads said he'll kill anyone comes looking. If I hurt myself again, try to leave here, he'll go to my house while my mama and papa are sleeping, and he'll kill them, my sister too."

Jason's voice broke then, his sibilant whispers broken

by a squeak in his throat as though he were stifling a scream.

"Told Sonny I had a pet rabbit. He told Dads. Dads said he'd skin my rabbit right in front of me, I don't behave."

"I think Dads is full of shit," Russ said.

He could hear a hissing through the hole that turned to a sustained sniggering.

"Better not let Dads hear that sass," Jason said when he'd recovered. The blue eye was crinkled at the corner.

"Fuck him and the horse he rode in on," Russ said, face creased in a grin.

More sniggering through the plaster.

"The boy before you was bad. He sassed Dads back like that. Bit someone too. I heard fighting, then he was gone."

"He talk to you?" Russ asked.

"All the time. I liked him."

"What was his name?"

"Trevor."

22

The Red Lantern Lounge squatted at the end of a strip of storefronts in what was, officially, downtown Haley. The only other stores without soaped up windows and realtor lockboxes on their doors were a nail salon and an antique store. The corner druggist, the children's clothing store, the hardware store and sandwich shop had all been swallowed up and shuttered with the arrival of the big box nationals out near the interstate.

The sky was darkening at half-past eight, the streetlights beginning to blink on. This time of the evening, the streets were empty except for a couple of kids skateboarding on an empty lot where the Haley House Hotel Inn had stood for a hundred years. A guy was walking a dog that was taking an interest in each and every parking meter along the curb.

The salon and antique store were long dark. Only the wavering aura of the Red Lantern's neon offered any color against the gloom of the evening.

Levon pulled the Avalanche into the lot of the Church of God's Light two blocks down from the bar.

Instead of approaching along the main drag, he walked north from the church lot toward the shadowy residential streets that ran behind the downtown strip. The houses were quiet, lit from within by the blue pulse of televisions. A dog barked from a backyard as he passed along the sidewalk that buckled in places where the roots of old oaks had undermined the concrete.

The homes that lined the streets were singles, old Dutch colonials and newer split-levels. Levon remembered thinking that this neighborhood was home to rich families with their big back yards and fine lawns. Since the Toyota plant closed fifteen years ago, the blocks had changed. Most yards had chain link fences with gates. The cars and trucks parked along the streets and in the driveways were older models where years before they'd have been the latest Corollas or Tundras. A few driveways had RVs or trailers parked in them—folks helping out kin in hard times.

Levon turned the corner to walk west until he reached the street that would take him behind the Red Lantern. The bar had a lot behind it surrounded by vinyl fencing. There were only six cars parked there. One of them was the Dodge Ram with two brand new tires shining under the guttering pole lamp that illuminated the lot.

Teddy Lee told Levon he'd find the two men he was looking for here most nights. "Sack" Price and Harley Yales used a booth in the Lantern as their home office. Teddy thought they might even own the place. It had all the signs of a front; cash business with few patrons in a town that progress, and the years, passed by.

Back at the meeting house in Sugar Run, Levon had taken Teddy's phone off him and pulled one from the pocket of the unconscious man on the floor of the meeting house. There was no trusting his cousin not to warn the men inside the bar. In the end, he let Teddy live but made him promise to leave the county, leave Alabama, and never let Levon see him ever again. Teddy agreed to every demand.

Still, Levon shot all four tires flat on Teddy's truck and took off back for the township road in Albert's 4Runner, which he plowed up to the switchback to the abandoned cabin atop Cooper's Rise to save himself the long hike back. He left the Toyota there to drive his Avalanche back down the ridge to the county road and Haley.

There was an open service door at the rear of the Red Lantern. The sounds of a working kitchen came through the screen door. Levon approached, his 1911 tucked against his waist now. A hammerless .38 revolver with the bird's bill butt rested in the deep pocket of his farm coat. The smell of fried potatoes and stale beer greeted him as he slowly drew the sagging screen door open and eased it closed again behind him. There was a corridor lined either side with cardboard beer cases leading past a cold locker and into a larger tile-walled kitchen, where a Hispanic man in a hairnet and apron dumped fries from a basket into a steel bin.

The man looked up with little interest as Levon stepped past him between the steam tables for the double swing doors that led to the main room up front. He gave Levon an "I just work here" shrug. Visitors coming in off the rear lot must have been an unremarkable event. Even so, Levon kept eyes on him as he shouldered the swing doors open.

The main room was all knotty paneling and soft

lights. An old Rock-Ola jukebox played some guy with a pronounced twang singing about good times and bad times he probably knew nothing about. The long bar was empty except for a pair of regulars in gimme caps, smoking and talking low, eyes locked on a flat-screen TV slung up above the rows of bottles. A woman tended bar; a bottle blonde dressed twenty years younger than her age. She leaned back on a sinktop, playing with her phone, alone in the world.

Three men sat in a back booth with empties and dishes smeared with ketchup before them. Levon recognized the broad back of Sack Price and the bobbing head of Harley Yales seated across from him next to a heavily mustached guy in a denim jacket.

Yales looked up with idle curiosity at the newcomer, his eyes growing wide as he recognized the man who cost them an afternoon at the Goodyear. Reading the surprise on his partner's face, Price struggled to turn his bulk without success.

Levon drew level with the opening of the booth, standing three paces clear. He rested his hand easy on the butt of the automatic in his waistband.

"Hands on the table," he said.

With a dark look, Price did as he was told. Yales followed his example. The third man made to object. The Colt came out of Levon's jeans to sweep in a sharp arc, the barrel striking the mustached man across the bridge of the nose with an audible pop. The man sputtered, spraying blood from his nostrils.

The two locals at the bar lost interest in the sports panel show they were watching and shuffled for the street without looking back. The blonde behind the bar leaned forward to lay her phone atop the Formica surface and stepped back to watch what came next.

"You find your cousin?" Price said.

"I found him."

"Bet he had a story to tell."

"That's why I'm here. I want to hear the rest of that story."

The mustache began to speak up, wanted to make his goodbyes, struggling to keep the tears from his voice. Levon delivered a hammer blow to the man's forehead with the butt of the automatic. The man drooped across the table, spilling bottles to the floor.

"What he told you was bullshit," Yales said, speaking up for the first time.

"Shut the fuck up, Harl," Price snarled.

"You need to pay attention to me. One of you is gonna tell me what you did with that boy," Levon said.

"Or what? You gonna hurt us? You gonna make us talk?" Price sneered the words, glancing to his partner, who snickered.

"No," Levon said, thumbing back the hammer on his Colt. "I'm not going to hurt anyone, but I am gonna kill one of you."

Price and Yales looked to one another.

"That would be the one who doesn't tell me where the boy is," Levon said.

23

Levon dragged the inert body of the mustached man to the floor before ordering Price and Yales to slide their asses, hands in view, out of the booth.

He ordered them to the floor where he stripped them of wallets, keys, and that shiny revolver he'd taken off the fat man earlier in the day. Price had a thick wad of bills bound with a rubber band in his pants pocket. Yales had a neatly folded aluminum foil packet of dusty white crystals. Levon stuck the revolver in his waistband and the keys in his pocket.

"Where's the Glock?" he asked.

"Never found it," Yales mumbled.

"You should thank me," Levon said. "Sit up now and pull off your boots."

As they did so, Levon backed to the bar where the blonde watched him with wary eyes. He set the wallets and wad of cash on the bar top.

"You know what that is?" he said.

"Best tip of my life," she said.

"What're you gonna do after we leave?"

"Close up and mail in the keys." A secret smile played across her face.

Levon stepped to the two men still seated on the floor.

"Pick up your boots and head for the back door. Fingers laced on top of your heads."

He followed them through the kitchen. The man at the sink watched the parade with wide eyes; his hands remained busy scrubbing at a stock pot in the steaming sink.

Out on the lot, Levon motioned them toward their truck. They hopped and groused, the rough surface painful through the soles of their socks. He took zip ties from his pocket and instructed Price to secure Yales' wrists at the small of the back. He ordered both of them to belly up to the tailgate of their Dodge.

"Put your right hand up on the bed cover," Levon said.

"What're you gonna do now?" Price sneered. "Take us out to the woods? Make us dig our own graves?"

"That would take all week," Levon said and shot Price through the back of the head.

Yales did a little stumbling dance, turning to see his partner slump to the ground. A dog started barking up the block. Half of the fat man's face was splashed across the back of the pickup. Levon stooped to scoop up the spent casing and put it in his shirt pocket. He noted the puddle spreading under Yales' stocking feet.

Levon gave Harley a shove.

"Move," he said.

Harley walking before him, Levon urged the other man across the parking lot that ran behind of the row of stores on the next block. They continued on to the parking lot of the church where Levon had left the Avalanche. Levon dropped the tailgate.

"Climb in," he said.

Harley did as he was told and lowered himself on his belly onto the lowered gate and wriggled awkwardly, like a spastic larva, until he was under the hard top that covered the bed. Levon raised the gate and locked it and stepped to the cab. He removed a rag from the center console and wiped blood from the 1911 and his gun hand before returning the automatic to the holster at the small of his back.

He drove off the lot, leaving the body of Sack Price lying two blocks north on the dark lot as the lights of the bar went out and the pole lamp died.

———

Harley Yales lay in the dark, jostled about on the shifting ribbed surface of the truck bed as it rolled from a paved to unpaved surface. He weighed his options and found there weren't many to choose from. If he didn't tell this guy what they did with Teddy Lee's kid, the guy was going to kill him. If he *did* tell him, then there were other people who'd kill him. Option two was the only real way out, the only one with a percentage of success. He'd just take off, make them find him, but then, they *would* find him and the longer they had to look, the more pissed off they'd be. He'd seen what they could do when they were pissed off. Letting this cowboy kill him tonight was looking like the better choice.

But that was a "maybe" then, and this was a very "real" now.

After all, this guy was not playing. Sack lying back at

the Lantern with only half his head was proof of that. This was a matter of blood, and these hillbillies took that shit seriously. A line had been crossed, and Yales was way over on the wrong side of it.

The truck came to a jolting stop that threw him against a fender wall. A cab door opened then slammed and the gate was dropped, allowing gray light in. The big man grabbed an ankle and hauled Yales out onto the gate. He lifted Yales to a sitting position with a fistful of slack shirtfront.

Yales looked about. They were parked in high weeds in the shadow of an interstate overpass. Truck traffic boomed past high ahead. His body could lie here for weeks before anyone but roaming dog packs found it.

"Where's the boy?" Levon asked. His face was in shadow, his body backlit by the glow from an industrial park somewhere the other side of tree line that ran along a service road.

"You ever hear of the Dixie mafia?" Yales said.

The question evinced a weary sigh from the cowboy rather than the gasp of suppressed horror that Yales had hoped for.

"You gonna answer all my questions with a question?"

"This is all about the Dixie mafia, friend. You heard of them?"

Levon recalled an office up in St. Louis. A wall safe, a heap of cash, and a man named Lou Bragg lying on a deep pile carpet with a fist-sized hole punched from his head. That was a matter of blood too. The men who killed his brother had to pay the price for that.

"You're telling me that I'll be in a whole new world of trouble for all this."

"You hurt me, and those boys will be all over your ass."

"I told you I wouldn't hurt you," Levon said.

"Then why you think I'll tell you shit?" Yales was shivering now, from fear or the chill of the night air on his soaked crotch.

"Because I'm gonna let you hurt yourself."

Yales blinked, nose wrinkled, and head tilted like a confused hound.

"I can lock you back up in the truck bed and just drive around a few days, you going cold turkey in the dark. When you're about to crawl out of your own skin, you'll tell me whatever I want for a taste of rock."

Yales' mouth turned to ash. He could feel his brain squirm at the prospect of going clean. His joints began to hurt at the thought of it.

"It was jus' business, you know. Your cuz owed us for services rendered. He was makin' good with the only collateral he had."

"Collateral."

"The kid was good for $10K. We moved him on for fifteen."

"To who? Who'd you sell the boy to?"

"Dan Sherwood. They call him 'Dads' 'cause he was a coach once. Football and shit."

"Where do I find him?"

"I dunno. We did the deal at the mall lot. Didn't go to any house. I don't know where he lives."

"Where's the boy then?"

"How the hell I know?" Yales was trying to sound defiant, but it came out as whining. "I don't know what these pervs get into. Maybe he kept 'im, maybe he sold him on like we did. They have networks for this shit."

"That's all you have."

"That's all. You gonna let me go now?"

Levon shot Yales twice through the chest with his revolver. Returning to the cab, Levon drove away, leaving the body in the weeds.

He had a name now.

24

Kenny Poole opened his eyes to a kaleidoscope of lights playing across the ceiling and walls of the dark room around him. He squeezed his eyes closed only to have the light replaced by a galaxy of stars swimming behind his lids, and his nose hurt, hurt real bad. He couldn't breathe through it, the nostrils plugged.

He lay a while on his back, eyes closed and breathing through his mouth, trying to remember where he was when he lost consciousness. He tasted fried onions and hops on the back of his tongue. The scent brought back the memory of the Red Lantern. His mama always said that smells held memories better than the ears or eyes ever could.

When he opened his eyes again, the lights were still there, A swirling blue and red aurora moving in a steady pattern projected through the front and side windows that faced the street. There was a fist pounding on the front doors and a hand trying the lock. He knew those lights. He knew that arrogant knock. There were cops outside.

Kenny rolled himself deeper in the shadows along the line of booths. He tried to crawl but raising his head brought on a wave of dizziness. On his way into the dark he rolled through a pool of spilled beer. He wiggled himself across the greasy tiles to a place under the booth table where he'd be out of sight from anyone peeking in through the windows.

He lay there listening and could hear a sound from the back of the place. A fist pounding, and then someone tried the service door that led to the kitchen. They gave up after a while. The lights remained, but no one was getting in.

While he stayed put in his hidey hole, Kenny ran an exploratory hand over his face. His mustache was stiff with dried blood. There was more crusted around a gash in his forehead. Even a gentle touch to his nose sent a lance of white-hot pain through his head. The knuckles of his hands weren't skinned, so it wasn't losing a fight that put him down.

Someone had kicked his ass. Some sumbitch came into the Lantern and sucker punched him. He lay his head back on the cool tiles and tried to recall who that might be, but it was all hazy and hard to get a focus on. In truth, he couldn't recall coming to the Lantern at all, though it was a familiar haunt. Last thing he could remember was having a fight with Lacey back at the house, but the sun was up so it had to be hours ago. Maybe that memory wasn't even from today. No clue what the fight was about. Lacey yammering in the kitchen and then out to the yard, where she followed him bitching about some damn thing, and him telling her to go fuck herself and driving away, and winding up here, he assumed.

A tinny voice from outside interrupted his memories, the radio from one of the cop cars, the bored voice of a female dispatcher.

Testing his ability to remain conscious, Kenny raised up on his elbows with a wince. He lay that way, taking sips of air until the vertigo passed. Kicking with his feet, he wriggled out of the booth, boot heels squeaking on the tiles. With great care, he braced a hand on a booth bench and rose to one knee. The pain in his head rose from a dull ache to a sharper stabbing then subsided back to constant pressure behind his eyes. When he levered himself up to a standing position, he heard voices at the front door, followed by a metallic jangle and a key rattling in the locks.

On the tiptoes of his boots and suppressing an agonized moan, Kenny made his way around the booths to the alcove at the back of the bar and into the single stall men's room. A bar of light came under the door as someone flipped the switches on. He took a seat on the commode and leaned forward to listen to the muffled exchange going on in the bar. He thought he recognized Judd, the day bartender, talking. The words weren't clear, but it sounded like someone was asking questions and Judd was answering.

Kenny grew bored, sitting and working at listening to the conversation going on out of range of his hearing. He pulled a handful of toilet paper off the roll and raised it to his nose to blow his nostrils clear. Thick clots of blackened goo exploded into the wad of TP. The relief of having his breathing passage cleared turned to a crushing wave of nausea at the sudden change in the cranial pressure brought on by Kenny's ill-considered nose blow. The vertigo returned with a rush, and Kenny felt the tiles shifting beneath his feet. His seat on the shitter was as precarious as that time he sat in the saddle of a mechanical bull at the state fair.

He'd never recall dropping unconscious off the toilet to slam his head into the stall door, alerting the cops outside.

When he next woke up, it was under bright lights in a bed at an emergency ward, his wrist cuffed to the raised bed rails.

25

Sonny brought Russ breakfast on a tray even though it was dark outside. Soggy cereal swimming in too much milk, and orange juice in a glass with a cartoon character on it, and, in a little plastic cup, another white pill. Russ lay with his back to the room, knees drawn up to his chest. Sonny set the tray on the dresser and made to leave.

"I don't want to take them anymore," Russ said, turning over.

"They're good for you. It's medicine," Sonny said, standing in the open doorway. The sound of the television came from downstairs, police sirens and squealing tires.

"I'm not sick."

"You're hurtin'."

"Only gonna get hurt more."

"You can't be this stupid," Sonny said. "You could make this easy, but you won't."

"That what you're doing? Making it easy on yourself?"

"Trouble with you is, you have a choice, but you keep making the wrong one."

"I can't leave here."

"That's not the choice I'm talking about, dumbass. Your choice is between giving Dads a lot of shit or just going along. Only way it's gonna get better for you is to go along."

"I can't." Russ felt a heat rise up his neck with the words. His eyes were hot, burning.

"Then he'll take the choice away from you. Won't change what happens to you. Nothing can change that. You're here now, and that's all there is to it." Sonny turned to step into the hall, his hand drawing the door closed.

"You can leave," Russ said.

The door came to a stop, Sonny's fingers gripping the edge.

"You can leave. Why do you ever come back?"

The door slammed shut. The locks clicked into place. Russ was alone again.

26

Having horses was fun until it became work. Everything had a price but, over the summer, the girls had fallen into the routine of feeding, watering, mucking, letting in, and letting out. Three horses and a goat looked to them for care, and they took it seriously.

"What did that boy say to you?" Hope said from where she was forking through the hay of Penny's stall to fill a muck bucket with droppings.

"Nothing you need to hear," Merry said. She was filling the rubber water buckets from a hose.

"He insulted you?"

"He's just stupid, okay? Forget him."

Hope was quiet as she hauled the bucket from the stall into the center aisle. They both worked in separate stalls, carrying forkfuls of manure to tip into the bucket.

"It was...*espantoso?*"

"Scary," Merry corrected.

"It was scary coming here to the USA," she said.

"I guess so." Merry thought it was understatement. Esperanza, as she was then, had been sold by her family for less than the price her new father paid for her pony. She was smuggled north and passed from one set of rough, uncaring hands to another until she wound up with a pair of men who were using her to shoplift, and probably grooming her for worse when she was a few years older.

"Yes. Scary. It is always scary to do something new, to come to a place that is not your home. Everything is new and strange," Hope said.

"You're not so scared now, are you?"

"I still have dreams sometimes."

"But you're happy here."

"*Sì*. Yes. So happy."

"Until today. Until that boy," Merry said.

"I was worried that people here would not like me. The men who owned me told me that the gringos hate brown people, people like me. That if I tried to get away from them, I would be hurt or locked in a *prisión*."

"You know that's not true. You're safe with us. You're our family now."

"Today, that boy reminded me of what I need to be *espan*—scared of." Hope fell silent.

Merry stopped work to go to the stall door. Hope stood leaning on the handle of the fork. Her face was tight with worry, a contrast from the cheery chatterbox she'd been since they left the school.

"What is it? What do you need to be scared of?" Merry asked.

"People like me," Hope said.

———

Merry woke up when she saw the headlights sweep across the windows of her bedroom. She padded from her room on bare feet as quietly as she could. *It wasn't necessary*, she thought, as Hope lay dead to the world in the other bed.

The first day of school had been exhausting for her new little sister. Mostly it was the excitement that wore Hope out. She talked all the way home and all through dinner, slipping into Spanish when English failed her. Uncle Fern said she sounded like she'd been vaccinated with a record needle—a joke he had to explain to them both. Except for the moment in the stable, Hope was in a sustained state of elation. Merry was surprised that Hope dropped off to sleep as early as she had, going silent mid-sentence to fall into a deep, motionless slumber.

The bluetick hound pup rose from where he was curled on a rag rug at the foot of her bed. He followed Merry from the room, nails clicking on the hardwood floor.

She went downstairs to find her father in the mudroom, washing his coat in the stand basin there. He was scrubbing at it with a brush and soap.

"You came back late," she said from the doorway.

"What are you doing up?" Levon asked, hanging the dripping coat over a drying rack.

"I wasn't sleeping so good. I wanted to see you before I went to bed."

"Sorry. I had a few things to see to."

"I called over to the Hamers. You weren't there."

"You checking up on me?"

"Just wondering where you were all this time."

"Doing a favor for my cousin Teddy Lee."

He'd moved into the kitchen, rooting in the refrigerator. She took a seat at the kitchen table, idly scratching the bluetick between the ears. The dog's tail beat a rhythm against a chair leg. Levon began building a sandwich on the counter.

"This have to do with Trevor disappearing?" she asked.

"I told him I'd look into it," Levon said as he layered ham, sliced turkey, and cheese onto slabs of mustard-slathered bread. "How do you know about that?"

"You have his laptop." She shrugged. "I know how to search a browser history."

"Smartypants, huh?" he said, setting the sandwich plate on the counter before pouring a mug of coffee from the percolator on the counter.

"That's cold by now," Merry said.

"It's okay. Cold coffee's still coffee," he said and took a seat.

"You having any luck finding Trevor?"

"I have a name, a man who might know where he is, only I don't know where the man is."

"Maybe I could help."

"Maybe you ought to get to bed. How was your first day of school?"

"It was good. My social studies teacher is a bore. I made friends with a couple girls."

"And Hope?"

"Daddy." Merry's eyes gleamed. "I never saw her so happy. It was like Disney World for her."

"How would you know?"

Merry tilted her head.

"I never did take you to Disney World."

Merry made a *phht* sound.

"Look, you better get off to bed. Second day of school is when the work begins, if it's still the same as when I went."

"A million years ago." She smiled.

He winced. "A billion years ago, it feels like."

She hugged him around the neck, and he held her close, savoring the moment. A quick peck to his cheek and she was off up the stairs, the bluetick loping after to take up his station at the foot of her bed. *And Fern thought that was* his *dog*, Levon thought.

————

Merry woke in the morning to lose the race for the bathroom to Hope. The scent of frying eggs and toast rose up the stairs and she made her way down, the hound pup by her side. The hound joined the Jack Russell who was already seated by Fern, begging with his eyes. Uncle Fern was working at the stove and her father sat at the table, the laptop open and a coffee, now steaming, by his hand.

"You're up early," she said as she snitched a corner of toast off the plate next to Levon.

"Never went to bed," he said and pulled the laptop closed.

"You want eggs, honey?" Fern said from the stove.

"After I get back. It's my turn to let the horses out," Merry said. She rose to go to the mudroom for overalls and Wellies. She stopped by her father, placing a hand on his shoulder.

"You have any luck?" she asked.

"Not a lick. This guy doesn't want to be found.

There's a few things on him but it's all old news. No current address."

"You need to find him to find Trevor?"

"Yeah."

"I know someone who's good at finding kids," Merry said on her way to the mudroom. "I'll bet she can help you."

27

The county DA made good on his promise to shake a CID team out of the state.

Sheriff Elmo Struthers came in Monday morning to find deputies Stivers and Breem sipping coffee in the squad room with Diane hovering with a glass pot to offer refills.

"You two look like shit," he said, and they did. Both men had bloodshot eyes with dark circles beneath. Their cheap suits looked even cheaper with the knees and elbows creased with wrinkles.

"Dispatch sent us out last night on a homicide up in Haley," Ben Stivers said.

"Haley? The staties usually take those calls," Elmo said.

"*Downtown* Haley. That taproom on the main street," Jack Breem said.

"Hell, that's one place I wish *would* close." Elmo huffed. "Who's dead?"

"Guy named Orlando Price," Stivers said. "Long

sheet for B & E, drunk and disorderly, possession and statutory rape of a minor."

"Sounds like someone did the county a favor. Any witnesses to this act of public service?"

"Place was shut up tight, but we found some loser passed out in the shitter. Lot was empty 'cept for the victim's truck," Stivers said.

"We know the loser?" Elmo asked.

"Name's Poole. Kenneth Fuller Poole. We've run him in a time or two. We got him in custody over at the ER."

"Person of interest?" Elmo recalled Kenny Poole. He'd been busted for aggravated assault a time or two and spent time with the county over some B & Es a couple years back.

"Yes, sir, Sheriff. Bill Quaid's waitin' there for him to regain consciousness."

"I'll head over there and speak to Poole myself," Elmo said. "What time was this?"

"Took the call little after 9:00 PM. Got there around half past," Breem said, reading from his phone.

"And the place was closed? You need to look up the owner."

"Did that." Stivers again. "He was home from the day shift. Said he had a girl on until closing. We drove out to the trailer park where she lives. Trailer was there but her and her car were gone."

"The closet was empty," Breem added. "Looks like she packed in a hurry."

"And Price was bootless," Stivers added.

"How's that?"

"His boots were off. Pair of brand-new ostrich Tecovas lying by him."

"Stay with it awhile, okay?" Elmo said. "Probably just

a falling out between dogs, but first go home and get showers and some sleep."

Both men hauled themselves out of their chairs to do as they were told. Diane offered the sheriff some fresh brew, but he declined.

"Two men up from Montgomery to see you, Elmo," she said as she went to replace the pot in the coffee maker.

"Where are they?"

"Waiting in your office."

"Shit, Diane. I needed to know that right off."

Elmo made his way into his office, offering apologies as he entered.

Two men in suits far better than those worn by his deputies waited for him inside. One occupied the visitors chair while the other opted to stand, pretending interest in the framed photos on the wall. Two mugs of Diane's poison sat together, untouched, on his desktop.

An older Black man in tan slacks and a summer weight sport jacket stood to introduce himself as Lieutenant Bruce Soames and his partner, a fit-looking white guy in his thirties, as Sergeant Andy McBride.

Soames had the moves and posture of a man who'd been a long time in harness. He had the kind of sad eyes that let you know he'd seen things in his years with the state. Elmo imagined Soames had come up from highway patrol to state detective the long way, taking courses on his own time and own dime, jumping through the hoops and taking the tests and kissing the right asses. It was the twenty-first century and all, but this was Alabama. While no one would hold a Black man back, neither could he expect any special favors.

In contrast with his partner's deliberate, "it'll get

done when it's done" vibe, McBride had a feral energy that he was making an effort to tamp down. Elmo knew the type, a man on the make, building a rep for himself for better things down the road. He'd be a major in the AHP by his fortieth birthday and retire a colonel. He was a careerist, and the kind of cop the sheriff had long ago learned to be wary of.

Hands were shaken all around. Soames was top dog by seniority and experience and would be taking lead on the Russell Loomis disappearance. The older man would be setting the pace and Elmo appreciated that. While the woman he sent in tears from his office on Friday wanted results fast and results now, turning the county upside down to find her son was not logistically possible. The lieutenant would be as thorough as he could be with the resources of the state behind him.

"I think you'll find it ties into some other disappearances we have up here," Elmo said.

"We got a running start on this, sheriff," McBride said. "I read the files over the weekend. The lieutenant read them on the drive up here."

"You might have some commonalities here in these cases," Soames said as he retook his seat. "But, with this little evidence, it's hard to draw a pattern."

"Kids run off." The younger man shrugged. He remained standing.

"I know that. Hell, we got crimes happening to kids younger and younger all the time," Elmo said from behind his desk. "Overdoses, assault, murder, rape. The girls are worse than the boys sometimes, but you get a feeling, you know? And this Loomis boy doesn't feel like a runaway."

"Your secretary said the mom's been in," Soames said.

Thank you, Diane, Elmo thought.

"She has. She's not the only one," Elmo said. "We got others gone missing inside the past twelve months. Eighteen months. All boys. All between seven and twelve. None of them are custody cases. All are in-county, up on the northern end near the state border."

"I saw that," Soames said. "I think we need to look across into Tennessee while we're at it, see if there's anything like this going on there in the nearby counties."

"Won't that bring in the Feds?" Elmo said and watched the two state men exchange a glance.

"Not if we ask real nice and real quiet." A fleeting smile crossed Soames' face. "The last thing any of us wants at this stage of the game is help from that clown show."

"You bring Washington in on this, and we'll get nowhere fast," Elmo said. "This is hill country we're poking around in. We need people to talk to us."

"I may not look it," Soames' smile was more genuine this time, "but I speak fluent hillbilly. Was raised up in Pickens County."

"That'll go a long way." Elmo returned the smile. "You let me know what you need from me, and I'll make sure it happens."

"To start, directions to the Loomis house," McBride said.

"And a place on the way that has a decent cup of coffee," Soames said.

28

"Jolene, a little help here."

Betsy Ritter stood bracing the door of her office open with her hip in the basement of the courthouse. The brass plaque on the door read: E.A. Ritter, Juvenile Advocate. Her arms were piled with a stack of files that looked to weigh more than her ninety pounds. In addition, she had a paper bag from Panera and a cardboard tray of coffees balanced atop the pile. Her canvas boat bag swung free from her forearm.

Her assistant, Jolene "I ain't no one's secretary" Bivens raced around the desk to rescue her boss. She stooped low, being a good head taller than the woman in the doorway, to take the files and takeout in her own arms. She turned to set them on the edge of her desk.

"Any calls?" Betsy rooted in her boat bag and came up with a pack of nicotine gum. She broke two pieces free of the foil and popped them in her mouth. She was quitting, again; only eight days off her two-packs-a-day Kools habit and not to be trifled with.

"Wallace called from juvenile court to remind you of the hearing this afternoon," Jolene said, scanning Post-Its plucked from the colorful array stuck to her monitor. "The garage called to say a transmission repair's gonna run $500.00. You have two new case assignments, some kid down in Briggs stole a tractor, and an arson case in New Temple."

"Alleged," Betsy said, eyes closed as the sweet release of nicotine invaded her system.

"Yeah, sure, everyone's innocent." Jolene shrugged as she set out the sandwiches and cardboard soup cups atop her desk.

"Pyros give me the creeps. Church burning?"

"Bandstand over at Possum Run Park."

"That thing shoulda fell down years ago. Anything else?"

Jolene pulled a last sticky note off to read it, a blue one.

"A Lee-von Cade. Says he'd like to talk to you. Says you helped his daughter a while back."

"Helped with what?" Betsy took a seat in a visitor chair and unwrapped a sandwich.

"Didn't say."

"He leave a number?" Betsy said around a mouthful of chicken salad.

"Said he was driving down to see you in person."

"But not about what?"

"Said he'd tell you when he saw you."

"What's he sound like?" Betsy took a long sip of life-giving caffeine.

"For *real*," Jolene said and took a bite of her sandwich.

Betsy returned from the hearing room in the courthouse annex to find a man seated on the bench that stood against one wall of the reception room. He stood when she entered, towering over her. He was dressed like he'd come off a construction site in work jeans, cotton shirt, and scuffed Timberlands. Something, and not just the high-and-tight haircut, said "soldier" about him.

"This is Mr. Cade," Jolene said from behind her monitor.

"Levon." He offered a hand.

"Betsy," she said and took his hand, or rather, as many fingers as she could grasp in her child-sized hand.

"I only have a few minutes," Betsy said. "But come on through."

In her closet of an office, cramped with files, books, and cartons, Levon laid out with military precision what brought him to the county seat. The disappearance of his cousin's boy. The shadow of suspicion falling on this Dads character. Betsy's suspicions were confirmed; this guy had been downrange.

"I remember your little girl," Betsy said. "She's a tough one. Smart too."

"She speaks very highly of you, ma'am. Thanks for your kindness to her."

"She got a shitty deal. I hate seeing kids treated like that, like pawns."

"Which brings me to my reason for being here."

"Levon, my job is to advocate for children in trouble with the law. The boy you're talking about is a possible *victim* of a crime. I'm not the right agency for this."

"The police aren't doing much of anything. Clock's ticking for Trevor."

"Did you think of giving what you know to them?"

"I don't really want to get in the middle of anything with the sheriff's department."

Betsy nodded. She recalled Meredith Cade's history well; a clear case of the system abusing an innocent,z and there was a deeper sense that her father wanted as little to do with the authorities as possible. She grew up in Mobile and went to schools up north, but Betsy had seen her share of this man's part of 'Bama. Describing people like the Cades as independent and wary of authority didn't begin to cover it.

"So, what is it you're looking for here?" she said.

"You have access to information I don't." He nodded toward the ancient desktop tower and boxy monitor on her desk.

"What would you do with that information?"

"Find Trevor. Bring him home."

That meant finding this man, Dan Sherwood, an unspoken understanding passed between them.

"I have his name. He was a teacher?" She was entering the name.

"Until he resigned five years ago. That's where I lost him."

The initial hits on Sherwood gave few particulars. He taught PE at Oakes Area High School for twelve years before resigning his position. He coached football and basketball. Graduated from Wake Forest. There was no apparent job history after him leaving Oakes. His residence was listed as being in The Terraces, a subdivision in the northwest corner of the county.

"You check this address?" she asked.

"A family's renting it. Has been for three years. They pay through a real estate management service."

Dead end. She broke out a fresh rectangle of nicotine gum to join the wad she was already working. She stood to allow her to see Levon over her monitor.

"Look, if this guy's involved in your cousin's boy's disappearance, then I'm guessing that has something to do with the issue that had him resigning. Just a wild-ass guess on my part. That means there might have been charges made."

"There would be a court record or arrest report."

"Don't see it. That would be a public record and nothing's here. He's not on the sex offender registry. He's never had a run-in with the law other than a DUI twenty years back."

"My intel is solid. I know this guy had contact with Trevor. Might still have."

"I believe you." She did too. His level of certainty was there in his eyes. She wasn't about to ask what made him so assured.

"If Sherwood likes kids, if that's what made him quit teaching, why isn't it on his record?"

"Because we're dealing with the teacher's union, the good old boys, and whatever associations this guy might have that protects its own. There's a code of silence here the mafia would envy."

"He has to be somewhere."

Jolene knocked politely on the frame of the open door and poked her head inside.

"You have your tractor thief and firebug to eval, Betsy," she said.

"Alleged, my dear," Betsy said with a wry smile. "We have company."

"I'm taking up your time," Levon said, standing. Jolene nodded behind him and retreated.

"Hold on," Betsy said, tapping keys and looking at the screen to write something across a legal pad.

She tore the sheet off and handed it to him across the desk.

"This is the county site where you can look at property tax rolls," she said. "They're public records but you need a password. I wrote mine under the web address. I'll change it on Friday, but you have until then to use it. If this Sherwood owns property, he'll be listed with further contact information."

"This should help. Thank you," he said and nodded his head to her before leaving the office.

"Give that girl of yours a hug from me," she said as he departed.

Betsy took a sip of her coffee and winced. It was lukewarm and tasted nasty in combination with the gum. She picked up the relevant court papers from the printer tray and placed them in her boat bag. Before standing to take off for her meeting, she sat a moment, leaning back in her chair to tap her teeth with the end of a pen.

She had no doubt in her mind that the man who just left her office would find the boy he was looking for. When Betsy was the worker on his daughter's case, she'd looked into Levon Cade's background. What she found there were mysteries far deeper than the ones she uncovered in her search of the vanishing coach's web presence. For close to a decade, this man didn't seem to exist, and she was never clear on where he was when he was absent from his daughter's life a year or so past.

The ghost of a chill rose up the back of her neck as

she considered her part in this. There was a realization that she might have helped in the recovery of a missing and exploited child. All well and good and let justice be done and blah blah, woof woof, but there was the feeling, with her simple suggestion of a path to take, that she had set a hunter on the trail of his prey.

29

"I told those guys. I told the doctors. I told the nurses. I told everybody," Kenny Poole said from his hospital bed. "I didn't see nothin'. I don't remember nothin'."

"You were there," Ben Stivers said from where he stood at the end of the bed.

"I was there, and I weren't there." Kenny shrugged, rattling the handcuff that connected his wrist to the bed rail.

"You can't remember anything."

"Doctor says I might not *ever* remember last night. I got a concussion."

"What's the last thing you *do* remember?"

"Jack shit, I was fighting with my girlfriend over some shit. Next thing I know I'm on the floor at the Lantern. Then I wake up here."

"You don't know who you were with at the Lantern?"

"I know I was with some fucker who coldcocked me."

The sheriff let out a deep sigh.

"Orlando Price was found dead on the lot back of the Lantern," Elmo said. "Shot through the head."

"You mean Sack?"

"A truck was left behind. It's registered to Harland James Yales. Both Price and Yales were associates of yours, right?"

"We had a beer now and then. You think Harley killed Sack?"

"Not if he left his own truck behind."

Kenny's brows knitted as his thoughts wandered, making his headache worse.

"You're a material witness even if you can't recall anything."

"But I ain't a suspect, am I?"

"No. Test shows you haven't discharged a weapon any time recently."

"So, I can go?"

"Doctor tells me they want to keep you till at least tomorrow morning. You took a line drive to the head, son."

"Okay then, how 'bout taking these off?" Kenny lifted a hand to draw the cuff chain tight.

"I'd feel better if you stayed in place for now. Can't have you wandering around in your state."

"I gotta piss and shit in a pan?" Kenny pouted.

"You're lucky to be alive." With that, the sheriff placed his business card on the rolling tray by the bed and left the room.

Kenny let his head fall back on the pillow, his skull feeling like it was being pressed in a vise. He thought about ringing again for a nurse. Only there was no reason to, as she'd only tell him they couldn't give him any painkillers for an injury like this.

Much as it hurt to think, he couldn't help himself.

He was at the Lantern with Sack and Harley when he

got poleaxed. Was he there on business or just having beers? Probably just beers. Made sense he'd come to the taproom after fighting with Lacey. He tried to remember what they were fighting, about but he never listened to that bitch much on a good day.

So, he'd wound up at the Lantern in the afternoon and was still there after dark, and wound up sitting with Sack and Harley. They would shoot the shit, telling each other lies. He was more a friend of Harley's than he was of Sack's. That Sack was a miserable son of a bitch with a real mean streak. Most times he just worked hard to make Kenny feel stupid. Kenny put up with it because Harley was a pal going way back to when they were at juvie camp together, and because the two were always into something good and sometimes needed a lookout or a driver.

Who's the stupid one now? Kenny thought. *Who got their smart-ass head blown off?* Most likely, Sack mouthed off to the wrong hombre. That gave Kenny a warm feeling. Lacey said it was karma when life came around to bite someone in the ass. Well, karma ended Sack, only what did Kenny ever do to karma to piss her off? Why'd *he* have to end up cuffed to a bed with a splitting headache?

He thought back to the last time he'd seen Harley and Sack, the last time he could remember. It was maybe a week ago at the ABC up on the highway. Harley was there on his own looking like he was buying out the whole store. Kenny had stopped in to buy some scratchers for himself and a sixer of hard lemonade for Lacey. Harley was there in line with a cart loaded up with four cases of chilled Heinies, a quart of Maker's, a fifth of vodka, and some mixers. The checkout girl was stacking up cartons of cigarettes on the counter as Harley pointed out the brands he wanted.

Always generous when he was flush, Harley paid for Kenny's sixer and lottos. Kenny went out to the lot to help his friend load the cases into the back of Harley's Ram. Harley broke open a carton of Marlboro Blacks and tossed Kenny a pack. They lit up to shoot the shit, sitting back on the dropped tailgate.

"What'd you get into?" Kenny asked him, having to shout as a semi thundered past on the interstate.

"One-time deal me and Sack made," Harley said, blowing a stream of smoke that drifted over the lot.

"Looks like it was sweet."

"Don't know about that. Made me a little sick."

Kenny turned to Harley who was studying the lit end of his cigarette as if there were answers in the smoke.

"Some hillbilly prick was into us on a loan," Harley said after taking a long drag. "Only collateral he had was his kid. His son. We took him for ten large off the loan and made another five selling him on."

"The kid? He gave you his little boy as payment?"

"It's all business. Just money, is all."

Kenny didn't ask who bought the boy. He already knew who'd pay that kind of money for a child and why.

"Shit, man," Kenny offered.

"Hillbilly pricks, you know?" Harley said and flicked the butt away across the lot, his face tight and eyes hard.

Thinking back on that conversation led to other thoughts that created little stabbing pains behind Kenny's eyes. He pressed his head back into the pillow and wished the drip leading into his arm was morphine instead of sugar water. He wished he had a hard lemonade. He wished he had a smoke. He wished they'd let him the hell out of here.

He thought he knew why he got coldcocked now, and why Sack got killed and Harley left his truck behind, and he knew who he had to tell about it.

It shit-sure wasn't the sheriff.

30

Gray dawn light came in through the window over the sink. The Jack Russell snored softly where it lay sleeping, curled against the dozing bluetick that shared the dog bed in the corner of the kitchen. Fern was up shuffling in his socks, half awake, to start the morning pot of coffee.

"You stay up all night staring into that thing?" he said. Levon was leaning at the kitchen table, eyes on the screen of the open laptop.

"No," Levon answered, eyes moving as he read. "Went to bed at one after getting nowhere. I was hoping all this would make more sense in the morning."

"Does it?"

"Starting to."

Fern set down a steaming mug before each of them before settling into a chair across from his nephew.

"I been looking into what we talked about before," the older man said, squirting a generous stream of honey into his mug from a little plastic bear.

"What was that?" Levon tabbed a key and hissed a curse between his teeth.

"A still, I mean, a distillery, you know, getting licensed and making some homebrew."

"What did you find out?"

"That it takes a shitpile of paperwork before I can even light the fire under a thumper. A wonder anything gets done with the local, state, and federal crowd of whores coming with their hand out."

"Yeah," was all Levon said. Looking at the endless rows of names and numbers on the county's property assessment site, he felt his uncle's frustration.

"Not sure it's worth the trouble, nephew. I'd rather take my chances cooking mash up the holler."

Levon took his eyes from the screen to regard Uncle Fern idly turning a spoon in a coffee mug.

"You don't have to deal with all that mess, Fern. You hire a lawyer to work it out for you, pull permits, and guide you through the swamp at the county seat and down in Montgomery."

"That takes money."

"We can cover it."

"I need a business plan."

"That's only if you were going for a loan. I can finance the whole thing and set you up. I'll bet there's a building open in Colby that'd be perfect for your setup."

"You're forgetting the whole reason I ever brought this up," Fern said. "You can't just go spending money like a drunk Comanche. You need something to put on a tax return to explain where all this cash is coming from."

"Guess you're right." Levon nodded.

"I can draw up the business plan and we'll present it to the banks. It's a pain in the ass, but I can work it out."

"Jessie did the same to start her vet practice. She could help us pull it together."

"I'll call her today, if it's okay with you," Fern said.

"Fine by me." Levon returned his attention to the laptop screen, but didn't miss the fleeting smile on his uncle's face at the mention of Jessie Hamer.

"You finding anything out on Trevor?" Fern asked as he stepped to the counter to top off his mug.

"This Sherwood owns a lot of properties, only none of them appear to be his residence."

"Man's got to live somewhere."

"Not so you'd know it from what I'm looking at. The best I can do is a post office box in Barker." Barker was a one-gas station town down the pike well west of Haley.

"You were away when they let him go." Fern returned to his seat. "He nearly took Oakes to state finals the year before."

Levon wasn't surprised his uncle had the dope on a local high school's football record. People south of the Mason-Dixon followed school ball the way the rest of country followed the pro leagues, college and high school both.

"What did you hear about him resigning?" Levon said.

"Not a whole lot. Barbershop rumors and bullshit." Fern shrugged. "Some whispering that he might have liked little boys."

"The school would be looking to bury that."

"When I was a kid, they'd've found him swinging from a tree."

"That's not how it's done these days."

"Don't get me started." Fern rose from the table to attend to the dogs who were now awake. The bluetick stood swaying, tail wagging. The terrier turned circles on the tile. Fern opened a plastic tub to scoop them each a bowl of kibble.

Levon turned back to the laptop. The web address Betsy Ritter gave him led to the county's property tax and assessment roles. Daniel Howland Sherwood owned nine properties without mortgage, liens, or any other encumbrances on them. He paid a grand total of just under $7,000.00 a year to the county in school and property taxes. His bill went to the post office box in Barker. There had to be a tax return filed with the state and the IRS, but Levon had no idea how to access that ,outside of calling in a favor from one of his many contacts made during his time downrange. One phone call would get him Sherwood's full record, only he wasn't about to do that just yet. Mostly because his favor bank was near empty. Partly because he wasn't anxious to reach back into that world. He'd give his search a day or two on his own before turning to former contacts at the agencies.

Cutting and pasting the addresses of the recorded properties to a map site allowed him to explore each one from satellite images. Each one had a house of some kind on acreage. They ran from five to forty acres with everything from log cabins to larger four-bedroom structures, former farm lots along with wooded acres. They were all in the more rural areas of the western end of the county, and two into the next county over. Probably rentals. The sat images showed cars or trucks parked at most, but the images would be months, even years old, and provided no clues to who occupied the places now.

One or more of them could be residences for Sherwood. The options were clear. He could visit each one to see if Sherwood was there, but he wouldn't want to start asking questions. He had no real authority to do so, and didn't want word to get back to his quarry. If the former coach got spooked, he might disappear for good. Levon also didn't want anyone recalling that a stranger was around asking after the landlord. He could stake out each property, hoping the man might show, or he could watch the post office in case Sherwood came to pick up his mail. Both ideas were probably a waste of time.

He had photos of the man from dozens of newspaper reports on his team's championships, training, and various awards events. In each, Sherwood was smiling alongside players or other teachers and coaching staff. He was a big guy with a broad face and the build of a man who was once fit but was letting age take its course, a jock with an impressive record as a wide receiver at Wake Forest. The pictures were a few years old, but Levon was confident he'd recognize the man on sight. He could assume the hair might be thinner and gut broader now, but the man was a celebrity in his corner of the world. Odds were, he'd done nothing to change his appearance.

A sudden burst of music exploded upstairs. The girls' clock radio. Feet hit the floorboards above them.

"Damn," Uncle Fern said, eyes turned to the ceiling. "Remember jumping outta bed like that in the morning?"

"Long time gone," Levon said and closed the laptop before standing and putting it under his arm.

"You leaving?" Fern asked.

"I'm gonna get a jump on looking at these properties. You mind running the girls to school?"

"Sure. You gonna be back in time to pick 'em up?"

"I'll call." And Levon was gone, the dogs charging out with him as soon as the screen door was open.

31

Rowena found herself in the middle of making Trevor's bag lunch again. This time she got as far as spreading the mustard on the bread for the ham and cheddar sandwich he liked best. On two mornings since he went missing, she got as far as making the sandwich, a baggie of apple slices and writing his name in Sharpie on the bag. It was a force of habit—finish making breakfast and make her son's lunch. The girls had refused to carry bag lunches since fifth grade.

She dabbed at her eye with a napkin and leaned on the granite-topped counter until the weakness in her legs subsided. She managed a smile and wave as the girls bounced past for the front door to head out to the school bus stop. The doorbell rang as she was sweeping the Guldens-smeared bread slices and mascara-stained napkin into the trash bin. This wasn't one of the housekeeper's days. She checked her eyes in the hall mirror before opening the door.

Two cops, Black and white, stood on the flagstone steps holding up badges and apologizing for the early hour. They introduced themselves, but Rowena forgot their names as soon as they said them.

"No need for that," she said and welcomed them in. She was already made up and dressed. It was a habit she'd fallen into since the day Trevor didn't come home. It was her way of being ready for any eventuality in case the phone rang with news good or bad. She owed her son that much at the very least.

"I don't know what I can tell you that I didn't tell the other police," she said once the two men had settled at the kitchen counter after refusing her offer of a drink.

"No thank you, ma'am."

"We're with the state and generally, we like to start from the beginning rather than take on where the county left off," the older man, the Black detective said.

"Sometimes, they're not as thorough as they need to be," the younger man said. Good-looking cop with an expensive haircut. Rowena thought about excusing herself to run a brush through her hair.

"Anything I can do," she said. "It's about damned time someone took this serious." "Your sheriff requested it," the black one said. "There's been a couple of other missing boys in the area."

Rowena drew in a sharp breath. Tears started in her eyes again.

"We're not saying there's a pattern," the younger one said. "We're looking to find or eliminate similarities with the other cases. Your boy most likely has no connection to the other boys."

"I just want him back home," she said, drawing a napkin to her running nose. It came out without a thought. She wasn't following what the detectives were saying at all. Their presence was a reminder that this was real, that this nightmare was actually happening. The daily routine of her life helped her function moment-to-moment, while the disappearance of her boy continued to occupy her thoughts on a subconscious level. The Xanax in the mornings and bourbon in the evenings helped too, but having these two very serious, very dour, very professional men here in her kitchen brought it all into keen focus. Trevor being missing wasn't a prank or tantrum or a childish whim. It was a *crime*, and her son was the victim.

"We're going to do everything in our power to make that happen," the Black detective said. His voice was calm and caring, admirable qualities of practiced empathy and assurance.

"Maybe we could start by looking at Trevor's room," the younger one suggested. "Then we could ask you some questions we have for you when you're ready."

Rowena poured herself a mug of coffee while the two men found their way upstairs. She sat at the counter resisting the urge to fortify the dark roast blend with a tot of Booker's until they came back down to the kitchen.

"We saw a cable for a computer," the younger detective said. "Did your son have a desktop or a laptop up there?"

"He did. One of my ex-husband's cousins came by and took it with him," she said.

"What was his interest here?" the Black one said.

"My ex is Trevor's father. He asked for his cousin's help finding Trevor."

"Is this cousin in law enforcement?" The young one.

"No, he's not." Rowena made a scoffing noise. The detectives shared a glance.

"We'll need that computer," the black one said. "Can you give us this cousin's address?" He offered her a pen and a page of a notepad he took from his jacket pocket.

"You can call ahead and get directions." Rowena wrote down Levon's phone number taken from her smart phone.

"Will the cousin surrender the laptop willingly, or will we need a warrant, Ms. Abruzzi?" the young one asked.

"You might need an army," she said with a crooked smile.

32

Betsy Ritter got out of bed hours before the alarm rang. It was one of those mornings where her thoughts wouldn't leave her alone in the predawn gloom, and it was too late to take anything. She gave it up and got out of bed to pad into the kitchenette of her apartment and snap on the coffee maker.

She sat at the café table, sipping a mug of strong brew as she opened her laptop and logged on. Her searches on Daniel Howland Sherwood did nothing but frustrate her.

"The hell with this," she said after a few fruitless entries. Betsy retrieved a crumpled pack of cigarettes from a kitchen drawer and lit one up using the fire stick that rested by her gas range. She leaned back on the counter and sucked in a drag of life-restoring tobacco. Luxuriating for a moment in the blue haze that wreathed her, she returned to the thoughts that woke her in the first place.

Those thoughts were about a friend from college named Naomi Rawlins. They'd been in the same circle at Samford where Betsy did her freshman and sopho-more years, and they remained in touch now and then. Naomi married a pediatrician and lived over in Tuscaloosa. S kept Betsy and others of their former circle apprised of the triumphs of her three endlessly remarkable children in four-to-five-page Christmas letters that arrived like clockwork each year in the week following Thanksgiving. Betsy wished her friend the best, but found the letters annoying as could be and, in recent years, had taken to dropping them in the trash unopened.

The reason why someone she mostly remembered for the time they drove into Montgomery to buy some weed kept coming to mind all the day before suddenly breaking into Betsy's precious REM time.

Naomi had taught at Oakes Area High until she got pregnant with her first baby, adorable little Jefferson who was, apparently, the most wonderful and talented boy ever born.

Her initial searches confirmed that Naomi's time as a geometry teacher overlapped the tail end of Dads Sher-wood's tenure as coach. She was there when he resigned.

Betsy let out her last glorious drag in a slow stream aimed at the ceiling. She ran the half-smoked Kool under the kitchen sink and dropped the butt into the disposal. Bars of gray light striped the living room through the blinds as she drained the last of her mug. In her bedroom, the clock radio was sounding, Patty Love-less singing of chains and regret.

She'd shower, dress, and hit one of the drive-thrus on the way to work. At a decent hour, after she assumed Naomi had packed her precious darlings off for another day of straight-A study and excellence, she'd give her old gal pal a call and do some catching up.

———

Naomi reacted to Betsy's call with a squeal of joy. It was as if no time had passed, and they were still at Evergreen Hall cramming for midterms and sneaking Jack Daniels past the RA in Snapple bottles.

They spent a few minutes catching up. Yes, her husband Joel was doing well in a shared practice and the children were doing great in school, with Caroline getting ready to graduate and everyone got over some kind of bug last week, you know how it is with kids in school. Betsy shared that, no, she was still not married, except to her job.

With a visit to the juvie center on her afternoon schedule, Betsy cut the catch up short with the reason for her call.

"You taught math at Oakes Area High near Haley, didn't you?"

"I did! I was there five years until I got pregnant with Sarah, and Joel and I moved to Tuscaloosa."

"Do you remember the gym teacher there? Sherwood?"

There was a sharp intake of breath on the other end. When Naomi came back on, her tone had changed.

"Is that son of a bitch still alive? Is he one of your cases or like that?"

"Informally. I'm making inquiries. So, you do recall him?"

"I was there when they made him quit."

"What can you tell me? The public record's not worth shit."

"All I know is what I heard, Bets and what I saw on my own. The man gave me the creeps. There always seemed to be younger boys around him, younger than his students or team members, always boys. I thought they were his own kids until I was corrected."

"What did people say about it?"

"You know. The same old stuff. 'Oh, that's just the coach' and 'He loves kids, is all,' that brand of horseshit when you damned well knew they knew what was going on. Everyone looked the other way because he was some kind of hometown hero or some shit."

"What happened to make them force him out?"

"It was terrible, remember, all's I know is what I heard. A little boy, Black kid, hung himself from the swing set outside his elementary school. You can only imagine the uproar that caused. People talking about lynching and all the rest."

"I can." Betsy vaguely recalled the story. It was a five-minute sensation in the news then died away to nothing.

"The police said it was a suicide. No doubt. Joel knew the doctor they brought in to assist the coroner. Said the boy had been raped over and over again over time. You know, anal?" Naomi whispered the last.

"Was there an investigation?"

"I guess, but nothing came of it. Then, two weeks later, Sherwood quits, right in the middle of the football season. And, you know what? There was more uproar over that than over that poor little boy. Can you imagine?"

"Unfortunately, I can." Her work as a professional child's advocate often brought Betsy into the heart of stories every bit as tragic as the one Naomi had told her. Even so, she felt her throat constrict at the thought of what the boy went through to force him to take his own life.

"And, just like that, he walks away."

"To what? Did anyone know where he went?"

"I heard he stayed in the county. He had a house there and some family still."

"What kind of family?"

"An uncle or an aunt, I can't recall."

"Where did they live?"

"I wish I could remember."

"Well, if you do, Naomi, I'd appreciate a call back."

"Sure. Sure," Naomi said in an absent matter, then continued, an edge in her voice. "You know what bugs me most about that whole thing back then? That none of the men did a damned thing about it. They turned a blind eye, the union and school board closed ranks around this bastard, and everyone moved on trying to forget about it when they should have taken a hand. Say what you want about the Old South, but there was a time, our daddies' time, when this would've been handled with a ball bat and a length of rope."

"I wouldn't worry about it," Betsy said. "There's still some of that Old South hanging on."

———

Betsy shared a hasty lunch at her desk with Jolene and was shrugging back into her leather jacket when the phone rang again. Jolene answered it and held the receiver out to her.

"Your friend," she said.

"I remembered something," Naomi said.

"Go ahead," Betsy said, snagging a piece of scrap paper from a pile on her desk, poised to write.

"The end of every football season, the coach would have a barbecue out at that house I told you where his aunt and uncle lived. It was on acreage, somewhere in the woods, west down the pike past Emery, way out there. I heard the teachers and some of the kids talking about it back then. The redneck event of the season and that."

"Any idea where west it was?"

"I don't, only that there were woods around it and a barn. I hope that helps some."

"It does, Naomi, and thanks."

Betsy spent every spare moment between her afternoon appointments deciding what to do with the information she now had.

33

A deputy came by earlier in the morning to take off Kenny's cuffs.

His head was still banging as he sat on the edge of the hospital bed and signed the forms for his release. The doc on duty, some dark man in a turban, told him that his brain was bruised, but not bleeding. He should lay off any drugs or alcohol and avoid driving for a while.

He called Lacey from the hospital lobby and ate some shit so she'd come and pick him up. She took her sweet time coming for him. He bummed cigarettes from some nurses and sat on the curb to wait. An hour passed before she pulled up with a pissy expression fixed on her face. The fight that drove him from the house two nights ago started up again before they were off the parking lot.

Lacey dropped him off at the first tavern they passed, a shithouse called The Wrangler that advertised "L VE MUSIC THURS 8" on a faded marquee sign, and roared off spraying gravel. Inside, the chairs were still up on the tables. The smell of pine cleaner covered the skunk smell left behind by years of spilled beer. He took a seat at the bar and the old fella left a sudsy sink to offer him a breakfast menu.

"Fuck that," Kenny said. "Gimme a double of Johnny Walker and a pack of Marlboros."

He sat smoking and sipping as he tabbed his cell phone to ask around after Dads Sherwood. He didn't have a direct line, just folks who knew folks who might reach him. After his calls were made, he moved to a booth and switched to beer, which he drank with a plate of eggs, bacon, and biscuits in gravy. He asked the old man for a couple of aspirin that he chased down with the beer. The pulse in his head died back a bit.

It was lunchtime and the regulars had been joined by a road crew in yellow vests by the time his phone rang. The caller ID read "Private number."

"Yello," Kenny said, his voice still raspy from the whiskey.

"You been asking after me." It was the coach.

"I got somethin' you should know."

"I know you?" The tone was flat, but Kenny could hear the promise of menace in it.

"I know *of* you. And, I know Sack Price, least I *used* to know him."

There was silence on the phone. Kenny could hear a TV in the background, women talking.

"You there?" he said.

"Where are you?" Dads said.

"Oldham Road north of the interstate."

"Meet me in an hour. Tell me what you have to tell me then."

———

Dads picked the Subway inside the Walmart in Haley.

Kenny spotted him in a back booth in the mostly empty restaurant. He'd met him only once a while back but would have known him, nonetheless. High school coaches, winning ones, were stars in their regions. Dads had been on the local news and in the newspapers plenty of times back when he was taking the Oakes Bobcats to all-county and once to all-state. He looked much the same, a little grayer, a little beefier, still a big sumbitch still and not a man to trifle with.

"Hey, Coach," Kenny said as he slid into the booth across from him.

Dads looked up from a half-eaten sandwich that sat atop spread paper. He had a large iced tea and was in the process of sweetening it with a splash from a silver flask that he returned to the pocket of his Birmingham Bulls starter jacket.

"What's your name?" Dads said, a professional smile that didn't reach as far as his hard eyes.

"Kenny Poole. We met once a while back."

"I coach you?"

"Naw. I played some b-ball for Ryerson. You kicked our asses."

The smile turned to a smirk. Dads pointed to the fresh butterfly bandages fixed above Kenny's right brow, the tape across his swollen nose.

"Who did to that to you?"

"The sumbitch I come to talk to you about."

Dads' eyes turned to anthracite.

34

Levon spent the day visiting some of the sites on Dads Sherwood's property list. He worked from his own list written on a yellow legal pad.

He checked a duplex and a two bedroom both in Colby, both rented out, and ten acres of wooded lot off the north county road that was an obvious investment buy waiting for the spread of new developments to raise its value. There was a hunting cabin set back off Dutton Wood Road that showed no sign of recent use, and a vacant row of stores halfway between Colby and Haley with "FOR LEASE" painted on the windows in yellow paint. The only activity there was some kids playing hooky to skateboard on the empty lot.

There were still six more lots on the list. All were farther out in the county and one across the Tennessee line. He'd cover them tomorrow when it was Fern's turn to pick up the girls and Levon would have the whole day.

It was a lot of holdings for an unemployed gym teacher. That raised questions of where Sherwood's funds came from. He was making some steady income from rents, but that left the question of where the money to buy them came from, and he had enough ready cash to pay $15,000.00 for Trevor. He was either into some other kind of illegal venture or these disappeared kids were a for-profit operation. The coach had turned his predilection for boys into a business. That meant he was tied into a network of kindred souls.

Whether or not he was connected to the Dixie mafia, as Yales had suggested, was doubtful. That was more likely a story Dads told in order to intimidate morons like Price and Yales into silence, but perverts had ways of finding one another, facilitated by the Internet. It was a strong possibility that Dads' revenue stream came from servicing that clientele. He either sold the boys on, or made them available. That last would mean he had to have a base of operations somewhere in the area. It was on the list of properties or perhaps off the books. Levon would exhaust the list and hope that one of them would turn up Trevor.

It was raining cats when he pulled up in front of the school to pick up the girls. They ran giggling through the downpour and piled into the back seat. The same Volunteer Grandmom from the other day, dressed in a yellow parka, waved them out of the line of waiting parents like a flight officer giving the go to a fighter jet off a carrier deck.

The girls kept up a rapid-fire exchange describing their day to one another. A mix of English and Spanish overlapped and was punctuated with giggles and exclamations. The wipers slapped back and forth, creating a rhythm to Levon's thoughts. He'd played with the idea of going out again after dropping the girls off. The heavy rain showed no signs of letting up, meaning he'd run into heavy traffic closer to Haley, and not reach the outer properties till after dark. He decided on staying in and getting an early start in the morning.

The brand-new cell phone mounted on the dash buzzed. He'd stopped by the Walmart the day before to join the twenty-first century with the cheapest phone on the rack.

"Noise discipline, ladies," he said and tabbed the phone. "You've got Levon Cade."

A familiar voice came through the speakers.

"Betsy Ritter. I might have something for you."

"You're on speaker phone, Betsy, and the girls are here with me."

Merry leaned past her father to call out, "Hello, Betsy!"

"Well, hello, darling. You sound a lot happier than last time we talked."

"Sure am! Just wanted to say 'hi'." Merry dropped back into the back seat to whisper to Hope.

Levon took advantage of a stop at an intersection to pull the cell from its holder and tab the speaker option off. He pulled the Avalanche onto a lot in front of a Kubota tractor dealership to continue the conversation. He held the phone tight to his ear as the rain drummed on the cab roof.

"We're off speaker. What do you have?" Levon said, voice low.

"Sherwood inherited a property from Forest Manville, an uncle by marriage. It's west on Corinth Pike on acreage, big house and barns from what I know. Sorry I don't have more."

"I think it's on my list." It described a fifty-acre lot

with a five-bedroom house, barn and machine shed set back off an undeveloped road that bordered state lands, remote, the nearest neighbors miles away. It was first on Levon's list for the next day. An inexplicable sense of certainty, a sixth sense developed by years spent downrange, gave Levon a strange comforting feeling.

"Maybe you'll find him there."

"It feels likely."

"I guess I'll see it on the news," Betsy said. Her voice quavered in an uncharacteristic break in her usual professional calm.

"Only if you're prepared to believe bullshit," he said.

"Maybe you can tell me the real story when we're both in rockers."

She broke the connection.

"Is Betsy okay?" Merry said as Levon pulled off the lot for home.

"She just had some information she thinks might help me find our cousin."

"Told you she'd be a big help."

"You were right, as always, honey."

The rain fell heavy all the way home, creating a gloom that turned afternoon to evening. The dark sky and continuous torrent reduced visibility. Levon drove almost the whole length of the driveway before he saw the piece-of-shit Ford pickup parked on the gravel.

"Stay in the truck," Levon said and stepped out of the Avalanche.

Merry watched him walk to the house and up the porch. He reached under his coat in a move Merry recognized. He was loosening the Colt holstered in his waistband at the small of his back. She hushed Hope and both watched through the water streaming down the glass.

Levon found Teddy Lee seated at the kitchen table with Uncle Fern. They were sharing a pot of coffee. Teddy turned, startled by the squeal of the screen door.

"What did I tell you, Teddy?" Levon said, standing clear of the table.

"I couldn't do it. Got halfway to Arkansas and turned right back around." He looked it, too, eyes red-rimmed and skin gray with exhaustion.

"What do you expect to do back here?"

"Whatever you're doing, cousin."

"I'm looking for your son."

"I should be with you."

"I don't need your help."

"I need it!" Teddy said, voice rising. "And you need to let me!"

Levon studied the man. It was clear Teddy was stone sober. His eyes were wet and pleading but his mouth was hard and hands steady.

"You bring a gun?"

"Got a Remmy pump in the Ford," Teddy said, rising from his chair.

"Pour that coffee into a thermos, Fern," Levon said.

35

"When the shit's flying, you just stay out of my way," Levon said as he turned the Avalanche off the drive.

"I won't get in your line of fire," Teddy said. "I know the safest place in the world is behind you."

"As long as you understand that."

"I appreciate this, Levon. I do."

"This ain't nothing like a second chance I'm giving you. It's just not my place here to tell you what you can or can't do."

"It's my boy." Teddy's voice sounded strangled now.

Levon said nothing.

"I wasn't in my right mind," Teddy said.

"Don't start that shit with me. Don't even start saying it was the drink or the dope. There's no way back from what you did, Teddy. No way back and no blaming anyone but yourself. You're gonna have to stand before Jesus someday and shit like that will not fly."

"I know," Teddy said in a small voice.

"It's a long drive. Get some sleep. I need your shit wired tight when we get there."

Teddy nodded and slumped low in the passenger bucket. He surrendered to sleep after a while, the crown of his head resting against the glass.

———

Levon was familiar with the country around Dads' house. There weren't many corners of the county he hadn't hunted or camped. If the Manville house was on an undeveloped road, that meant it was probably set at the end of that road. A direct approach was not the best idea. The property listing described the property as in "the vicinity of Branch Creek Rd off County 90".

Teddy was still fast asleep when Levon pulled off onto the shoulder. The rain was slacking off as night came on. It was down to a fine, cold mist now. He pulled a well-worn county map from the sun visor and unfolded it on the steering wheel to find the section he wanted. He found Branch Creek where it left the pike and traced its length south, where it ended about five miles in. Somewhere in there, the undeveloped road cut in. He tugged the phone from its holder and opened a map program. He found Branch Creek and switched to satellite mode. Expanding the image, he found a narrow, single-lane roadway that snaked away from Branch Creek, going generally south-southeast for three miles following the course of the creek in a ragged curve. The unnamed road ended in a collection of buildings with metal roofs, a large house with dormers and a couple of additions, and a hay barn and some kind of longer garage building. It was nestled in a U-shaped clearing in the trees with ten or so acres of open ground behind it.

Levon refolded the map and replaced it in the visor.

He removed the back of his phone and took out the SIM card and snapped it in half in his fingers. The Avalanche pulled back on the road and, a few hundred yards along, Levon tossed the pieces of the SIM card from the window, followed by the phone itself another mile or so along. As he drove, he retrieved a new phone from the center console of the truck and placed it in the holder on the dash.

———

Teddy came awake when the motor sound died, and he realized they were stopped. He blinked as the dome light came on, and turned to find Levon rooting behind the dropped back seat.

"Get some coffee in you and stretch your legs," Levon said.

Teddy climbed from the cab, rubbing his face. It was full night and cold. The truck was parked at the edge of a gravel road surrounded by dark woods. He reached into the cab for the thermos and poured a cup that he downed in three gulps. Levon tossed him a pair of blue nitrile gloves.

"Where are we?" he said to Levon, who was handing him his own Remington 12-gauge.

"The woods back of the house we're looking for. This is a fire road that cuts across the state lands south of County 90." Levon handed him a box of buck.

"Okay. I hunted back up in here a few times with Jack Rudd and that boy Watkins. Where we heading?"

"We walk this way down through the trees till we come to the clearing. The house is the other side of it, maybe a quarter mile."

Teddy squinted to see the nascent glow of light coming from somewhere the other side of the trees.

"You got a handgun you don't mind me having?"

Levon handed his cousin his .38 snubby and a handful of shells. Teddy stuck the revolver in the back pocket of his jeans and the shells in the side pocket of his jacket. The shotgun shells went into the opposite pocket. Levon had the Mini-14 slung over his shoulder and extra magazines in the pocket of his barn coat.

"What are we expecting?" Teddy said.

"No way of knowing, but we're prepared for the worst."

"We have a plan?"

"We head on down there. Get your boy. Kill anyone who tries to stop us. Come back to the truck."

"With me behind your every step."

"That's important, Teddy. We stay together with you on my six."

"Whose house is it?"

"You remember Dads Sherwood?"

"The coach?"

"It's his house. The man has a history."

"Well, that ends tonight," Teddy said, and they walked from the truck into the woods.

36

"This bitch is one fine ride, Dads," Kenny Poole said behind the wheel of the coach's Escalade as they pulled off the Walmart lot. The low clouds that threatened all day had opened up, and rain swept across them carried on gusts that moved like surf over the feeder road that wove between the big box stores.

"Shut up and drive," Dads said from where he tabbed a phone in the passenger seat. He was only letting this moron drive his car because he needed his hands free to use the phone in private.

Kenny reached for the entertainment center mounted in the center of the dash and Dads slapped his hand away.

"Keep your goddamn eyes on the road," he roared.

Kenny turned back to the windshield with a hurt look on his face.

Dads had to agree with this dumb fuck, that the bastard that killed Sack Price might have something to do with the kid Price and Yales sold him. If that were so, then the trail would lead back to him eventually. With

Sack's asshole buddy missing, Dads thought it was a safe bet that the mullethead, whose name Dads had forgotten, had given him up.

The boy's name was Trevor Cade. He didn't remember Sack mentioning any names of relatives, next-of-kin. Only that it was the boy's own father who gave him up for forgiveness on part of loan. The father's name would be Cade, too. Was that who killed Sack? Did the father have seller's remorse and want his kid back now? Too late for that, Daddy-o.

Dads didn't have much more than that to go on. He called a few numbers in his contacts asking about anyone named Cade. It wasn't until he called Ricky Wagner down at the Indian Lake Inn that he found anything of use. Ricky was a listener and a talker and had worked behind the bar at the shitty little tavern on the lake for as long as Dads could remember.

"Used to be a Cade was a sheriff's deputy, but he died a while back," Ricky's voice said from the phone. "There's an old man Cade still lives out near Colby. Ran shine with his brother. My ma used to talk about them, wild pair."

"Is there a Cade still in the county?" Dads asked. "Has a son, maybe eleven or twelve?"

"Don't know one with a son. There is a Cade with a younger daughter. Last I heard he was back in Colby living with the uncle. Don't know a lot about him these days."

"Why not?"

"He left home out of high school. Joined the Army, or some shit. Was away a long time, but just moved up here from Mobile or Huntsville or somewhere else south."

That's the one, Dads thought. He pulled a scratch pad and Sharpie marker out of the center console.

"You know where this uncle lives?" Dads said.

———

Sometimes horses could be pure-D dumb.

Merry and Hope were out in the paddock in their oilskins in the downpour trying to coax a ton and a half of animals to come in out of the rain. Bravo and Whiskey shied from them each time they approached, and the pony followed the pair of horses wherever they went. There was just no way they could get close enough to grab a halter. As twitchy as they were, it would be a mistake to try and catch them that way in any case. The girls split up to try and get behind them at a safe distance to clap their hands together and shout in an effort to goose them into the barn.

In the toasty dry barn, the goat, formerly known as Junebug but renamed by Uncle Fern for a former president, stood on a hay bale bleating as if to express the superiority of goat sense over horse sense.

Merry spun the knotted end of a lead line in her hands and clucked encouragement to Bravo. The big gelding spun about and charged through the open doors at last. Penny followed at a trot, clopping into her own stall. Whiskey, sensing that playtime was over, stopped his gamboling to walk ahead of Hope into the barn where he stood with flesh ashiver as vapor rose from his coat.

The girls set about the work of cross tying the mounts and wiping them as dry as they could. The rain hammered down on the metal roof in a dissonant cadence as they groomed and watered and secured them in their stalls with feed for the night. Tricky Dick settled down on his hay bale, letting out the occasional gripe until his pan was filled with sweet feed and cabbage leaves.

Tired, soaked, and hungry, the girls closed up the barn for the night to head for the house at the far end of the yard. Merry turned to see headlights coming up the drive. She was not expecting her father back so soon. That wasn't his truck. She joined Hope under the shelter of the front porch to watch the car turn in the yard and come to a stop next to Teddy's Ford. A dark sedan. Men got out either side and, collars pulled up, trotted up the steps to the porch.

"We're with the state police," the taller of the two, a Black man with kind eyes, said. "Is there anyone home but yourselves?"

37

Levon and Teddy walked through the woods to the pattering sound of droplets falling from drenched boughs. It was cold enough in the woods for them to see their breath. After twenty minutes of downhill travel, they came to the edge of the trees. A gentle slope of high grass led down to a redoubt of trees five acres distant. A dome of light shone against the trees through the fog created by the misting rain.

Levon dropped to a knee, holding out a hand to halt Teddy's stride. Still in the shadows of the trees, Levon took a compact scope from the pocket of his coat and trained it toward the light.

The old farmhouse came into view through the 20X lens. A pole lamp turned the night to a warm gloom. The yard between the house, machine shed, and barn was fully illuminated under the glare. Parked in the yard was a collection of vehicles. Two pickups, an El Camino, and a Suburban shining beetle black in the cold light. A wisp of smoke drifted from the SUV, and Levon trained his scope toward it.

A man sat behind the driver's seat with the window partly down to allow smoke out. The glow of his cigarette revealed him to be a Black man with a shaved head. Too far away and at a bad angle to judge with any accuracy, but Levon guessed he was in his thirties. He played the scope down the side of the Suburban to read the license. Georgia plates. Government plates.

He lowered the scope to consider what he'd seen. Teddy made to ask a question and Levon gestured for him to hush. They were state plates, but not law enforcement. This wasn't a bust. It was a client. It was a safe guess that the man behind the wheel was an on-duty cop waiting for someone inside.

Once more, he lifted the scope to his eyes and swept the house looking for cameras. There was nothing on the walls or slung under the eaves. The windows were all shuttered or heavily curtained, allowing no light from within. The windows on the second floor were all barred. This approach was clear except for the waiting man.

"Is this the place?" Teddy whispered.

Levon nodded and stood up, replacing the scope in his pocket and unslinging the Ruger. He pointed to their right and moved low out into the clearing. Teddy followed behind and to his right. They trotted along the tree line until they were at a place where they could approach from the blindside of the man in the SUV.

The grass offered little cover as the earlier storm had mashed much of it flat to the sodden ground. They made the best speed they could crossing the field, taking care to stay at the edge of the waiting man's peripheral as well as out of the reflection area of the side-view mirror.

As they neared the car, Levon could hear soft jazz coming from the car's radio. He could smell the tang of the man's cigarette. He increased his pace. His booted foot made a squelching sound in the thick mud. The driver turned his way just in time to take the hard-plastic butt plate of the Ruger in the forehead. His head caromed off the door edge. The driver went limp.

Levon had the car open and the man out on the ground. He was dazed and muttering through spittle flecked lips. Levon lifted him in a chokehold until he went silent. While Levon patted the fallen man down, Teddy reached into the Suburban to hit the tab on the dash that opened the tailgate.

Under a navy-blue windbreaker, the driver wore a holstered Glock, radio, and handcuff case. In his pocket was an ID folder with his photo and a badge. John Coolidge, state highway patrol sergeant. Levon tossed the pistol and radio far out into the dark before cuffing the man's wrists behind him. With Teddy's help, they moved him to the rear of the car and lifted him onto the tailgate to roll him inside. Teddy closed the gate while Levon cut the engine before pulling the key and throwing the ring out into the field in a different direction than the pistol and badge.

Levon pulled a clasp knife from his jeans pocket and pointed to the other vehicles. Teddy nodded and unsnapped his own buck knife from his belt. They moved among the cars and trucks punching holes in the tires. The vehicles sagged on the gravel like animals settling down to rest.

Levon and Teddy raced across the wavering pool of light from the pole lamp for the back of the house. They were offered three options for entry: a kitchen entrance, a sliding door that opened onto a poured concrete patio, and a standard casement door that led into a vinyl-sided addition that jutted off the main house.

The wooden door into the addition was the best option. Levon climbed a set of creaking wooden steps to open the screen door and press his ear to the glass pane at the center of the door. The glass had yellowing sheets of newspaper taped against the inside. He could hear music from within, something electronic with a driving rhythm.

He brought the butt of the Ruger down hard on the doorknob. The lock popped, making the door swing in, creating a gap that allowed light out. Crouching low he levered the door open with the barrel of the Ruger for a turkey peek inside.

The addition was a summer kitchen-cum-storage room with stacks of Rubbermaid containers lined against kitchen cabinets. The source of light was from a ceiling fixture, the main kitchen in the main body of the house, with only two of its three bulbs lit. The music was louder now, coming from somewhere deeper inside the house. Levon turned to Teddy and waved for him to follow.

Guns raised, they moved through the kitchens toward the sound of the music. The main kitchen appeared to be unchanged since the 1950s, with peeling steel wall cabinets and an ancient electric range. The only thing new in the room was a Sub-Zero refrigerator and freezer looking like a visitor from the future against the rest of the vintage fixtures.

The kitchen exited into what would have been a dining room but instead had a pool table in place of the family setting. A tacky faux Tiffany lamp decorated with the Coors logo in plastic hung over the table. This room was dark and opened through an archway into a hallway that led to the foyer at the front of the house. It led along the side of a stairway to the right. Along the left wall were entrances to three rooms; one closed off with a door and two others with open archways like the one from the dining room.

The music came from the nearest room, accompanied by a pulsating light that reflected on the floor and far wall. It was the background music for a video game. Levon could hear the sound effects of revving car engines and squealing tires under the music. Holding a fist up to stop Teddy from following, Levon stepped into the archway with his rifle leveled.

A shirtless teenage boy with shoulder-length hair turned from a sofa to freeze when he saw the end of the rifle barrel trained at his head. His mouth went slack even as he squinted in disbelief. Levon could smell the sweet stink of weed in the air. A bong rested on the sofa by the boy. His eyes were red, lids swollen.

"How old are you?" Levon said in a low voice.

The boy goggled.

"I said, how old are you?" Levon stepped closer, the barrel inches from the boy's head.

"Fourteen," the boy said in a whisper made hoarse by the smoke.

"Get out of here and don't come back," Levon said between clenched teeth.

The boy leaped to the back of the couch, sneakers squeaking on the floor as he brushed past Levon, then Teddy, and raced from the house into the night.

38

"Do you have a warrant?" Fern asked, leaning back on the kitchen counter with arms folded.

"Do we need one?" the one who introduced himself as State CID Lieutenant Soames said, seated in a kitchen chair scratching the head of the bluetick hound. The hound's tail thumped on the floor in gratitude. Rascal, Fern's Jack Russell, possessed of a more suspicious nature, and sat in his dog bed eyeing the two troopers with a wary gaze.

"We were told he was working on his own to find this boy," Sergeant McBride said from where he stood behind Soames, raincoat open to reveal his holstered sidearm.

"Your nephew, isn't he?" Soames said.

"The missing boy is a cousin," Fern said.

"The boy's mother said that your nephew, Levon, took the boy's laptop computer," Soames said. "We're assigned to this case, and we really need to get a look at that."

"You mean seize it," Fern said, his expression

darkened.

"If that's how it has to be," McBride said.

"We've had more than our share of law up here poking around and turning things over. Gut-sick of all of it, you know? All's Levon's doin' is trying to help family. Can't you leave a man alone to do that?"

McBride looked to Soames who waved a calming hand his way. Sheriff Struthers had given Soames a heads-up that made Soames make a quick call back to Montgomery. It appeared that this Levon Cade had been the subject of a federal investigation, as well as receiving some interest from the state of Alabama on a variety of charges. It was all dropped months ago, and the files sealed, so as far as anyone knew, Levon Cade was a solid citizen minding his own business up in his own holler.

"We want to help too," Soames said. "And we have the resources."

"Where were those resources when we called before? Seems like all of a sudden, you're lookin' to do your jobs when a couple weeks back you couldn't give a shit."

"The county didn't call us in until now," McBride said. "This looks to be bigger than just Trevor."

"Do you think you can find him?"

The three men turned to see Merry standing in the kitchen door, a laptop held against her.

"Is that your cousin's computer?" Soames asked.

"Yes. Will it help you find him?" she said and held it out in her hands. McBride stepped across the room to take it from her. Uncle Fern's brow furrowed, and he looked at his niece with a look of deepest reproach.

"It'll go a long way," Soames said with a smile and pulled a folded form from the inside pocket of his raincoat.

"My daddy was only trying to bring Trevor home," Merry said as the detective filled out the receipt form and turned it to Uncle Fern who signed two copies with a huff and a grunt.

"We'll have a look at it and bring it back when we're finished," Soames said, returning one copy of the form to his pocket and standing.

"You better damned well see that you do," Fern said.

With a final pat to the hound's head, Soames turned to leave. McBride held the screen door open for him. They trotted out to their state car under the pelting rain. Merry watched them back away across the gravel and swing about to the driveway, all the while aware that her great-uncle was glowering at her. His frown melted into a grin.

"How'd I do?" he said.

"Academy award stuff," she said, returning the smile. "Browser history wiped."

————

The state car came to the rutted lane and turned onto the paved road to head back to the sheriff's office. It crept along the asphalt toward the curve that would carry them to the county road. The rain was coming down in sheets that drew visibility down to three car lengths.

Neither Soames nor McBride saw the Escalade pulled up under the drooping pine boughs along the roadside.

"That was damn sure cops," Kenny Poole said. "An unmarked, sure as shit."

"Fuck," Dads Sherwood said. "Fuck. Fuck. Fuck."

39

Sonny's sneakers were sodden and squishy by the time he reached his Nissan. He pulled the keys from his jeans pocket and yanked the door open only to bang his head on the cab frame as he slid in. It was then he realized that the truck was sitting low on flattened tires. He leaped from the truck in panic and turned to run to put the house behind him.

All of the vehicles in the yard were sunk down on their rims. Dads' Harley was in the carport, but Dads kept the keys to that on him at all times, his baby. Sonny glanced back at the house before turning to run into the field, to leave this place to the men with the guns. As he ran past the black Suburban, he heard a pounding on the glass and a dampened voice shouting from inside.

Sonny leaned close to the glass to peer through the tint. A Black guy was in the cargo area. He lay on his back drumming the soles of his feet on the glass. Sonny leaped back as the man lifted his head to shout at him, eyes furious with impatience. Sonny moved, slipping on the wet gravel, to the front end of the SUV to hit the release for the rear doors.

He swung the gate down and the man inside rolled over to face him.

"Kid, there's a key in my watch pocket," the state trooper said. "Fish it out before those fuckers come back."

Sonny found the small silver peg key in the pocket and helped the trooper to a sitting position, his legs hanging over the tailgate. He struggled with wet hands to get the key into the lock of the cuffs. The muffled thump of gunfire from within the house startled him and he dropped the key to the ground.

"Goddammit, kid!" the trooper growled.

He found the key where it fell on the ground and freed the trooper's hands.

The trooper leaped off the tailgate to shoulder Sonny aside and race to open the rear door of the Suburban.

"You gonna call for backup?" Sonny said, eyes on the house as more gunfire erupted from the house.

"That ain't how we're gonna play this," the trooper said, pulling a black rifle from a padded case that he'd retrieved from under the rear seat.

40

At the bottom of the steps, Levon gestured for Teddy to stay behind and moved up toward the second floor. The rifle held before him, he reached the top of the stairs and moved down the center of a long hallway that ran along the stairwell. It was lined on the opposite side with rooms. Each room had a heavier than usual interior door installed with multiple locks. A peephole was set in the middle of each door at eye level.

The hall was dark but for the warm glow of light coming from a partly opened door at the end. Levon could hear water running. Under that sound was the resonance of a man's voice echoing from a tile surface.

Using the end of the rifle barrel, Levon levered the bathroom door open until he had a view of the room. A wan-faced boy, no older than seven, sat naked in a tub of soapy water. By the tub sat a man on a stool, naked under an open bathrobe. The man sat stroking the boy's face with a sponge. His other hand was shifting in a rhythmic motion under his robe. He was cooing to the boy in a low voice between wet gasps.

Levon took the man to the floor with a stroke of his rifle butt. The man was dazed, moving over the slippery floor in an attempt to escape, the robe hiked up to expose his flabby rear. Levon followed, rifle trained. The man managed to turn over, sliding on his ass to put his back against the front of the sink cabinet. He looked up with dewy eyes, mouth slack with fear.

"Do you know who I am?" the man said in a gobbling stutter.

"How many more are here? How many like you?" Levon said.

"Do you know who I am?" the man repeated, a note of confidence rising in his voice.

Levon turned to the boy sitting in the tub watching. The boy's pupils were wide and black like the shoe-button eyes of a stuffed doll.

"Cover your eyes, son," Levon said.

The boy did as he was told, clasping soapy hands over his face.

Levon turned back to the now mewling man and drove the butt of the Ruger hard into his face. The man kicked and spasmed, bare feet squeaking on the damp tiles. Two more strokes and the man stopped moving. Levon threw a bath towel over the body. A crimson splotch spread across the terrycloth where it covered the crushed skull.

"What's your name, son?"

"Jason," the boy said.

"You can take your hands down now."

"How many other boys are here?"

"I only know Russell."

"Any others?"

"I don't know their names."

"What about Trevor?" Levon asked. "Is there a boy named Trevor here?"

"Trevor's dead," the boy said, voice quavering with a sudden chill.

An explosion of gunfire from downstairs. Once. Twice.

Levon left the boy to step into the hallway. Three rooms down, a door was flung open and a doughy man wearing only boxers and black socks stepped into the hall to look over the railing. Levon shot him center mass with a double tap. He moved quickly down the hall to put two more rounds in the man's head.

"Teddy!" Levon called.

"Yeah!"

"Up here!" Levon said and leaned over the railing. Teddy stood on the third step from the bottom, looking up at Levon, the shotgun in his fists. Sprawled belly down on the steps was what was left of a barefoot man. His khaki pants and a pullover were now sodden rags where two loads of buck had impacted.

"You find Trevor?" Teddy said, starting to climb the stairs past the corpse.

"Stop," Levon said.

Teddy froze where he was. Levon listened hard to the house sounds. Somewhere he heard footsteps.

"There's a back stairs," Levon said and turned from the railing. Teddy stumbled back down the steps to race deeper into the house.

Levon turned the corner at the end of the hall leading into an addition that was a kind of servant's quarters. Levon raced across the room. A young Black boy in a bed goggled at him over a quilt held up under the boy's eyes.

He shouldered the door open to a walk-in closet, then a half-bath, before finding the door to a narrow staircase that led downstairs to a landing that turned into a second flight of stairs to a doorway. The door at the bottom of the steps was open and the light from below revealed a figure leaping from the landing. Levon fired three rapid rounds after the man before charging down in pursuit.

Shouting voices came from below, Teddy and another man. The exchange was cut short by the boom of the shotgun followed by an animal howl.

Levon called out to Teddy before coming out of the bottom of the stairwell. A man lay on his side on the floor of the main kitchen. He was whimpering and holding hands clasped to the calf of one leg. Blood sprayed between his fingers. He was buck-naked and maybe in his thirties. A skein of tats covered his wiry frame running over his back, chest, and arms. The ink was hipster bullshit with Celtic patterns and rows of bold Chinese characters.

"I need a hospital," the man hissed between clenched teeth.

"You need to shut your fucking mouth," Teddy said, standing over the man to thumb fresh cartridges into the belly of his shotgun.

"Let him be," Levon said. "Keep watch."

Teddy stepped back to cast his eyes to the archway that led from the kitchen to the main house.

Levon crouched by the fallen man who was growing white with shock now. He spoke to the man in a low, reassuring voice.

"You answer my questions, and we'll get you treated," Levon said.

The man turned his head to meet Levon's eyes. The man's pupils quivered under the trauma that had come close to tearing his leg off. He managed a feeble nod.

"We found three other men in here. Is that all that was here?"

The man thought a moment, eyes darting.

"Three men and you. Is that right? Is that all?"

The man nodded.

"Where's Sherwood? Where's the coach?"

"He was here when I got here but left."

"When was that?"

"Earlier."

"When?"

"It was daylight, before it rained."

"How many boys are here?"

The man spasmed then. His eyes lost what remained of their focus. Levon gave him a tap to the face that restored his attention.

"How many boys are here?"

"Um. Um. There's the littlest one and the nigger kid, and Dean and some new boy. I ain't seen him."

"The boy with the long hair? Who's that?

"Sonny, that's Sonny. He's Dads'. He been here longest."

"Is Dads coming back tonight?"

"Don't know. Don't know."

The man was fading. His hand fell away from his ruined leg. The flow of blood slowed as his pulse weakened. Levon shot him twice through the head.

The shots were answered by a spray of automatic fire from somewhere outside.

41

"You and I are going to my place," Dads said to Kenny Poole from behind the wheel of the Escalade. He was driving now, squinting into the glare of oncoming lights turned to dancing halos in the falling mist. His eyes darted to the rearview mirror, looking for any swirling lights behind them.

"What for?" Kenny said. "I ain't in this with you."

"You can have this car. You know the commercial airport in Cumberland?"

Kenny shrugged.

"We're gonna head there after I pick up a few things. Then you take the car. I'll throw in some cash."

"Where you going?"

"Now why the fuck would I tell you that?" This dickhead was trying his patience like some of the dumb bastards he'd coached used to do. Couldn't remember the simplest pass play until you made them run it a thousand times.

"You got the papers to this ride?"

"What? You want to go to the tag place? Do a registration transfer? Sell it to a Mexican. Chop it for parts. Like I give a shit."

"Sorry."

"Trying to do right by you, doing you a solid, and all I hear is bullshit."

"Sorry, man."

"Just shut up a while."

They rode in silence for a few miles.

"We almost there?" Kenny said.

Dads' fists blanched white as he tightened his grip on the wheel. He turned his head from the road to look at Kenny. The other man read in those eyes a world of untapped fury and remained silent for the rest of the ride.

42

John Coolidge sent a pair of three-round bursts into the rear of the house to follow his initial long volley. He was squatted behind the cover of the Suburban's engine block, the M4 rifle trained around the window he saw the muzzle flash through. The kid with the long hair kneeled by him, body pressed against the car, eyes wide and shivering in the cold.

The house was silent. There was no movement and no return fire. Coolidge had no clear strategy here other than to hold his own ground. The Suburban had four flats, as did all the other cars he could see. Whoever was inside had their reasons to keep everyone right where they were. He had no idea what this was all about. Home invasion made no sense. Some kind of score was being settled here, most likely. Whatever this man, or these men, were after, they stopped at killing a state trooper. Though his head hurt like a motherfucker and the vision in his right eye was swimming, Coolidge knew he was damned lucky to wake up, even luckier this kid came along.

"How many men?" he said to the kid.

"I saw two." The kid's voice squeaked up an octave as he spoke.

That made sense. The reports from inside the house came from a shotgun and either a rifle or big bore handgun.

"Tell me about them," Coolidge said.

"White guys."

"What else?"

"White guys. What do you want? I only saw 'em a second before I ran."

"They say anything to you?"

"The big one asked me how old I am."

"What for?"

"Like you don't know what goes on in this house." The kid's eyes narrowed. His mouth twisted in a smirk.

Before Coolidge could respond to that, a load of buck turned the windshield of the SUV to white powder.

43

"Who's out there?" Teddy called to Levon from where he lay belly down on the floor of the kitchen.

"Quiet." Levon was down behind the cover of a chest freezer. He levered up to get one eye over the lid of the freezer. The glow of the pole light shone in beams through holes punched in the shutters. The glass pane at the center of the back door was starred with three holes.

From his memory of the yard behind the house and the placement of the vehicles parked there, Levon placed the shooter about where the car with state plates was. Somehow the trooper must have freed himself or had help. Now the man was armed with an automatic weapon and had the back of the house covered.

"Levon! Cuz!" Teddy was hissing as he dragged himself under the kitchen table. "We need to get outta here. That statie's probably already on the radio."

"He's not calling anyone," Levon said and ducked lower as more shots, in three controlled bursts, came through the back wall and windows. Bits of glass sprayed tinkling over the lid of the freezer to drop on him. He felt the impact of a couple of rounds that buried themselves somewhere in the contents of the freezer.

"What're we gonna do? We ain't found Trevor yet," Teddy said, sliding over the tiles to join Levon behind the freezer.

Levon cut him a look and turned away.

"I think I know where he is," Levon said. "We need to keep him there, keep his attention right here."

Teddy nodded eagerly. His pupils were pinholes in his bulging eyes. The adrenaline was up in him; he was nearly shaking with it.

"You get a shot off with the Remmy while I work over to a better angle," Levon said. "Give me a count of three."

Levon moved swiftly away from the shelter of the freezer into the greater darkness of the summer kitchen. Teddy counted off then leaped to his feet to fire the shotgun from the hip. The blast tore a shutter from place, filling the room with light from outside. The roar of it still in his ears, Teddy dropped to his ass and worked the pump to chamber a new shell.

He curled into a ball as a long volley peppered the back wall of the kitchen. Rounds struck dishware and glasses on the table, sending shards flying. Holes appeared in the doors of the steel cabinets with a metallic *plunk-plunk-plunk*. The lighting fixture in the ceiling burst to send a shower of glass particles over everything.

The firing outside paused as Levon reached a side window of the summer kitchen. The silence was interrupted by two more blasts from Teddy's pump. Levon stood, laying his rifle across the drainboard by a double sink, and took out his clasp knife. He placed a hand on the thick fabric of the blackout shade that covered the window above the sink. He pressed the shade against the glass and, with his other hand, made two cuts in the fabric in an inverted "V."

He dropped back into a crouch as the rifle outside sounded again in two abbreviated barks. There were crashing sounds from the kitchen followed by a new eruption from his cousin's shotgun. Levon raised up again and peeled back the point of his cut. The fabric folded down to reveal a triangular viewport in the shade. Through this, Levon could see the vehicles gleaming wet under the incandescence of the pole lamp. He sighted the Ruger through the triangle until he found the Suburban. A shape moved next to the front driver's side wheel.

Levon took in a breath, let it out, and waited.

44

The last shots from the house were low, spraying gravel where they landed somewhere off to Coolidge's left.

He loaded a new magazine into the rifle and rose to a crouch to fire over the hood of the Suburban, lighting up the back of the house near where he saw the twin flashes from the shotgun. The kid was curled in a ball by Coolidge, hands tightly clamped over his ears.

The way he saw it, there were two ways this was going to go. The men inside had to know they were outgunned and would try and slip away on the other side of the house. They might even be doing that now; one covering the other's withdrawal. The other possibility was that the men inside would try and wait him out.

That would be the bonehead play. The trooper had a number in Atlanta to call that would bring help, not official help, not any kind of state agency. The man he could call commanded a separate authority that dealt with things like this quietly and expediently.

Only, he'd want to hold off on that call. Coolidge

preferred to handle this himself, to soften the blow of what might look to others as a fuck-up. Hell, he was just a glorified driver. His badge was useful for smoothing out the bumps; for sidestepping questions and complications that might arise. No one said anything about an assassination. Nobody could expect him to have anticipated that Bumfuck, Alabama would turn into Detroit all of a sudden.

He'd give this bullshit another twenty minutes. If the fuckers inside wanted to play Alamo, then he'd make the call to the man in Atlanta.

The shotgun boomed out again sending a load of shot shrieking into the night sky.

He stood to return fire and the whole world went white.

───────

Sonny had his eyes closed and ears covered when he felt the weight of the Black guy collapse against him. He clawed at the gravel to pull himself free. There was a warm spray on his face. His hair was sticky with it. His nose and mouth were filled with the taste of copper.

He kicked his feet to push himself away. The Black guy lay limp against the wheel of the car, a crimson stain gleaming in the lamp's glare against his windbreaker. A snarling grin fixed on his face; teeth smeared red.

With a whimper, Sonny rolled away to leap to his feet and launch himself into the tall grass that spread away behind the house. He hooked left off the gravel lot and ran straight on for the trees. He gasped, drawing in air, expecting a shot in the back. The trees looked to be miles away, an impossible distance. The sawtooth tops of the pines atop the ridgeline shifted back and forth against the sky as he sprinted to them, wishing, praying even, that he would reach the sheltering dark before a bullet found him.

He promised himself that he'd run until he could run no more. He'd run until the sun rose and long after. He'd put that house behind him and run. He had no idea where or in what direction. He had no destination. He had no home. He had no place to go back to. He only knew that he would never come back here.

45

"The cop?"

"Yeah."

"Is he dead?" Teddy said to Levon who was returning from a trip out to the Suburban. He left the rifle behind to tell whatever story those who came to investigate wanted it to tell.

"He's dead," Levon said and entered the kitchen through the door held open by his cousin.

"We killed a cop."

"*I* killed him, Teddy. And that wasn't any kind of cop."

"Just thinking of the trouble we're in." Teddy was following Levon across the kitchen.

"Those boys need us," Levon said, opening the door to the back staircase. "Take the main stairs up and meet me."

Teddy trotted from the room.

Upstairs, they found the boy from the tub and the Black boy standing in the hallway looking at the body of the dead man in boxers and black socks lying in a lake of blood. They appeared to be only mildly curious, the Black boy touching the man's blubber with a bare toe. The boy from the tub had a bath towel wrapped around him like an outsized toga. The Black boy was in pajama bottoms and a T-shirt with a robot on it. The Black boy made to run for the head of the main stairs at seeing Levon, only to be caught by the arm by Teddy coming up from the first floor.

"The other boys," Levon said in a soft voice to the shivering boy in the towel. "Show me where they are."

"Where's Trevor? Which room's he in?" Teddy called from the top of the stairs, his hand locked on the skinny arm of the Black boy.

"Tell him, son," Levon said to the white boy.

"Trevor's dead," Jason said.

Teddy let out a howl, releasing his captive's arm and sinking down to sit on the top step. Rather than escape, the Black boy stood by him, watching the grown man crying into his hands. The shotgun rested across his knees. The boy reached out, stroking the back of Teddy's coat.

"Show me where the other boys are," Levon said.

"Yes, sir," Jason said and led Levon along the hall.

———

"Is this all of you?" Levon asked the collection of four boys standing in the hallway. Russell and Dean; two more white boys a little older than the others. Russell was having trouble standing on his own. He'd been heavily drugged, and his speech was mushy and confused.

Teddy remained where he sat down at the head of

the stairs, his face wet with tears. His mouth was still twisted in a rictus, eyes far away.

"'Cept for Sonny," Dean said.

"Older boy with surfer hair?" Levon said.

"That's him. He ain't here."

"He ran off."

"What about Dads?" Dean said, glancing at the corpse on the hallway carpet. "He dead too?"

"We didn't find him," Levon said.

At that, Russell came out of his torpor and made to bolt. He could only manage a stumbling gait and Levon caught him easily, stopping him with a firm hand to the shoulder.

"You're safe now, Russell. You're going home."

The boy searched Levon's face with a dull gaze, struggling to comprehend. Levon turned to Dean, who appeared to be less affected by what was going on. The boy's eyes were clear of drugs, though there was an emptiness there that Levon recognized. He had experience with longtime captives and knew the look of someone who'd surrendered all hope. These were no longer the eyes of a child.

"Dean, the other boys," Levon said.

Dean blinked.

"The other boys. What happened to them?"

"The cellar. They're all down in the cellar," Dean said, pointing through the banister rails.

"I want you to show me," Levon said, offering his hand to the boy. Dean took it and pulled Levon toward the head of the stairs.

"Teddy," Levon said. "I need you up. I need you focused."

Teddy looked up at his cousin and nodded.

"You stay with these boys and keep a watch on the driveway," Levon said.

Teddy's brow creased.

"That son of a bitch has to come home sometime and there's only one way in here," Levon said, making his way past Teddy, pulled along by Dean down to where Teddy's first victim still lay sprawled on the stairs.

His cousin stood then to rest the shotgun in the crook of his arm. Teddy motioned for the other three boys to follow him.

Down on the first floor, Teddy went to the double front doors to find them secured with deadbolts that locked from the inside. The keys were not in the locks.

"Where's the keys?" he called back to the boys.

"Dads has 'em on a big ring," Dean said.

"Cover your ears, y'all," he said and aimed the shotgun at one of the heavy brass locks. The boom filled the confined space. The buck bit pieces from the doorframe but did little more than scratch the finish on the chunky Schlage.

"Shoot the hinges," Levon called.

Teddy placed the end of the barrel against a hinge and blasted it from the frame. He did the same to the bottom hinge, and the door sagged away from the jamb. He kicked, and the two doors swung out until their combined weight tore them from the frame to crash down on the porch. Teddy placed himself where he could watch the driveway where it came out of the woods to cross before the house.

Levon turned to see the reinforced door that sat between the archway to the game room and the opening to a living room. It had a row of three deadbolts, and metal bands screwed in place in a latticework. The hinges were concealed inside.

"What's this?" he asked the boys. "Is this a room or a closet?"

"Dads never lets us see in there," Dean said.

"Is there anyone in there? Another boy?"

"Nah," Dean said, shaking his head. "He just keeps stuff in there."

"Let me see that," Levon said to Teddy, stepping forward with his hand out for the shotgun. He traded the rifle for the pump gun.

"You have some pumpkin balls in the mix I gave you," Levon said.

Teddy dug in his coat pocket and came out with a handful of red shells. Levon pumped the last round of buck from the Remington and slid the tube full of the heavy slugs. Three pumps and holes appeared in the doors where the lock cylinders were driven through the wood. Levon chambered a new shell and shouldered his way into the room to flip a light switch by the door. Levon entered the room with Dean peeping around the doorway after him.

"Always wanted to see in here," the boy said.

The room was a windowless closet, a cloakroom at one time. The rear wall was dominated by a tall gun safe. The side walls were lined with tall metal cabinets. There was no time to deal with the safe, but the cabinets were secured with simple padlocks that surrendered after getting slammed with the butt of the shotgun.

The cabinets had steel shelves loaded with double rows of labeled videotapes. The dates on the labels went back ten years as far as Levon could determine after a quick study. There were names on the labels. Some of them had a vague familiarity. Levon was certain he'd heard the names somewhere on the television or read them in the paper. There were no recorders in the tiny room. Levon didn't recall seeing cameras in any of the rooms upstairs. He'd need to find any recorders but first he had a task for Teddy.

"Change of plans, cousin," he called to Teddy.

Teddy turned back to him from the doorway.

"Go and get the truck," Levon said, tossing his key ring. "While me and the boys pack all this shit up."

His legs felt like lead, and he had to fight to keep his muzzy thoughts together. Teddy was exhausted after two days with little sleep beyond the fitful nap he took in Levon's truck. The adrenaline rush was over now. He felt a weakness in his legs and arms. His joints began to complain. The Ruger slung over his shoulder was getting heavier with every step. He wanted a cold drink and a warm bed in that order.

He had the truck in sight when an arc of faint light brushed the boles of the trees before him. There were headlights moving around the back of the house below. Teddy was torn for a moment, whether to run back to the house or head on for the truck.

A new rush of tension and fear drove him up the hill, legs pumping, for the Avalanche parked in the trees.

———

Dads saw the dark shape of a body lying by the Suburban as he swung around to park alongside, a Black man in a dark windbreaker lying half-seated/half leaning against the front quarter panel. Beads of glass spread over the gravel shone like diamonds in the high beams of the Escalade. He saw the silvery holes punched in the body of the dead man's ride.

"What the hell, man?" Kenny Poole, coming out of a stupor as Dads pulled back in reverse into a slewing bootleg that sent clots of mud up into the wheel wells.

"They're here, goddamn it!" Dads barked as he spun the wheel hard to point the frontend back toward the driveway.

"Who? Who's here?"

"Police! That sumbitch Cade! Somebody's here! Fuck!"

The headlights washed over the side of the house revealing a man walking along the verge of the drive toward them. White flashes of light bloomed from a weapon in his hands. The windshield starred. The pattern of shot holed the hood and sent a side view mirror flying away.

Kenny let out a gurgling wail before clawing his door open and tumbling into the dark, leaving a wide smear of blood on the seat. Dads stomped on the gas and fought the wheel around.

The truck rose on one side as the front and rear passenger wheel rolled over the body of his former passenger. The Escalade was off the road now and hydroplaning across the wet grass.

Dads threw the lever into neutral, and the SUV came to a rocking stop facing the rear of the field behind the house. The rear window collapsed into a shower of beads as he slapped it back in gear and stood on the accelerator to send the big vehicle forward. No particular direction in mind, he only wanted to put distance between himself and the fucker with the shotgun.

At first Dads thought the lights coming from the trees were a reflection of his own. But the shotgun had taken out both headlamps when it sprayed his front grill. He turned a hard right when he realized that the glow was from a second vehicle. Some kind of truck with big knobby tires was making for him, ahead of twin rooster tails of mud geysering high behind it.

Dads made as sharp an arc as he dared and felt a hesitation as his rear wheels spun in the slick goo he'd churned up. With a welp of pity for himself he dropped into a lower gear and shot forward on a course that would carry him past the house on the opposite side from the shotgun man.

A sudden jolt tore his hands from the steering wheel and slammed his head against the glass of his door hard enough to spiderweb it. He looked helplessly through the shattered windshield as the world spun around in a half arc before coming to a sudden stop that pitched him into the explosive embrace of the airbag erupting from the steering wheel.

In pain and in panic, Dads Sherwood snagged the door handle and rolled from the Escalade to the muddy grass, coughing on the powder from the airbag that fogged the air. On hands and knees, he scrambled to take cover behind the car while pulling a 9mm auto from the inside pocket of his starter jacket. He popped up over the hood just enough to see the pickup that had come to a stop where it slammed into his rear quarter in a violent pit maneuver.

There was still a figure inside the truck cab and Dads fired three snap shots. One round punched through the windshield. There was a roar from the truck. Whether it was pain or rage, Dads wasn't waiting to find out. He clambered to his feet and ran away at an angle that kept his wrecked Escalade between him and the truck. Off to his right he could see the shotgun man rushing across the field to intercept him. Dads fired at the man as he ran, the bullets wicketing into the treetops far beyond the running man.

The ground was slippery under his slick boot soles, and he fought to stay upright as he ran. The coach had not run like this since his college days and a painful stitch grew to an agonizing fire in his side. He bit down and kept on; body bent almost double to make it up an incline in the ground that led to the edge of the tree line bordering the field.

His leg went out from under him and, at first, he thought he'd stumbled. Then a lance of white-hot flame shot up into his groin and he looked down to see the meat of his shattered knee through a ragged hole torn in his slacks. Whimpering, he dropped on his belly to pull his bulk through the grass with the strength of his hands and arms alone. His pistol was gone now, torn from his grip when he fell.

A punch like the blow of a hammer struck him in the back and he flopped hard into the muck. He could hear the sucking sound of feet closing on him through the mud. Another punch accompanied by a sharp explosion and a flash of light. This time his other leg went numb under impact and he knew he'd be unable to go on.

A weight dropped on his back, shoving his face to the ground. His mouth filled with sludge, and he gasped to regain his breath. He felt the prod of cold steel pressed hard against the bone behind his ear. His ears filled with the wheeze of the man who kneeled astride him. He heard the click of a revolver hammer being drawn back.

"Hold up, cousin," a voice called.

"What for?" said the man on Dads' back.

"Maybe he has something to say."

"What the fuck I want to hear from this shitbag?"

The second man stepped closer. With his one exposed eye, Dads could see the pair of muddy work boots that belonged to the shotgun man.

"What about it, Sherwood? What's your life worth?"

"Anything, you fuckers. A thousand? Two thousand?"

"How about the combination to that safe?"

They found the safe. They found the tapes. He was holding a shit hand.

"How about it?" the man said again and placed the toe of one of those work boots on Dads' hand and began to apply pressure.

"All right! Shit! Fuck!"

The boot lifted off his hand.

"It's 65432 and the pound sign."

"That would have been my second guess," the shotgun man said after a *huh* sound that might have been amusement or might have been scorn, or both.

"Now, where do you keep the recording equipment?"

Dads fought hard to maintain his concentration. Gray dots swirled at the edges of his vision.

"The stuff off the cameras," the man said. The pistol pressed harder into the soft flesh of his neck.

"The TV room," Dads said, gasping. "There's a wooden cabinet back in the corner."

Dads felt the steel of the barrel end come off his flesh.

"He's all yours, Teddy," the man said and stepped away.

Teddy had three shots remaining in the .38 and made the most of them.

47

"Are you gonna be all right?" Levon said.

"Fucker clipped me. Hurts like a bitch," Teddy said, leaning on the Avalanche and clutching his arm. Blood ran down over his gloved hand from under the sleeve of his coat.

Levon lifted his cousin's arm to inspect it. Teddy hissed and winced. It looked like a through-and-through wound; the round entered above Teddy's wrist and exited at the elbow through a ragged hole in the cloth growing stiff with dried blood.

"We'll get you looked at." Levon opened the passenger door and helped Teddy into the cab. "Just keep it elevated as best you can."

"I'm gettin' blood all over."

"This truck is done anyway."

Levon got behind the wheel and drove them around the house, where he turned it and reversed to back up to front kitchen door.

"Stay here," Levon said, opening the door.

"Trevor's dead," Teddy said in a small voice.

Levon left him to drop the tailgate, then went to the busted-out doorway to find the four boys waiting for him inside the house. They'd already stripped the metal cabinets bare. The videotapes were stacked in cardboard liquor cases and bundled in Winn-Dixie shopping bags.

"Can you boys carry these out and load them in the truck for me?"

"Where's Dads?" Dean said. "We saw his car."

"He's dead," Levon said.

"You killed him?" the one named Jason said, his voice rising.

"He's dead. Doesn't matter who killed him," Levon said. "Now, will you do as I ask?"

The boys carried the bags and boxes to the Avalanche and began sliding them inside the bed. Levon went to the closet room and punched in the code. One side of the safe held a rack with rifles and shotguns. A few handguns rested in pockets on the door. The shelves running down the other side held ammo boxes. On the floor of the safe rested an insulated fireproof box that Levon pried open with the blade of his clasp knife.

Inside were some papers, a college ring, and a small cardboard tray of audio cassettes. He set aside the tapes and upended the box, spilling out thick bundles of cash wrapped with rubber bands that lined the bottom. He stuffed the cash into his coat pockets along with the tapes, and stepped into the hall.

In the room with the big screen, he found a wooden cabinet with swing doors on the front. Inside was a bank of three VCRs, all recording. He ejected the tapes from each and carried them to the front door to toss them with the others in the back of the Avalanche.

The boys stood quietly about the truck, shivering in

the predawn chill. Steven, the Black boy, was on tiptoes peeking in at Teddy sobbing in the cab.

"You gonna take us home now, mister?" Jason asked.

"I can't do that, son," Levon said. "Not after what we've done here."

Russell was stricken by his words, the color draining from his face. He clutched the sleeve of Levon's coat with a pleading look. Levon crouched down to speak to the boy eye-to-eye.

"You've been brave. You've all been brave, and you keep on being that way, okay?" Levon said and turned to the others. "After we've left, when we're out of sight, one of you count to one hundred then call 911."

"I don't know where we are," Dean said.

"Use the house phone and stay on the line. They'll find you. Tell them your names."

"They'll take me home?" Steven said.

"They'll take you all back to your families."

"What do we tell the police?" Dean asked.

"You don't have to tell them anything. I'd appreciate it if you forgot about me and the other man, forgot you ever saw us. I can't ask you to lie. That's up to you."

Dean nodded and the others followed his example.

Russell's grip remained fixed on Levon's sleeve until Levon touched the back of his hand. The boy let go and stepped away, turning his face and fighting back tears.

They stood watching as Levon closed and secured the tailgate. He climbed into the cab. They stepped in bare feet out into the mud of the yard to watch the Avalanche pull away down the drive and into the trees to vanish in the gloom between the pines.

"One...two...three..." Dean began, and the others joined in to count with him.

48

Soames parked their unmarked sedan along the edge of the rutted trail. He said a silent prayer they wouldn't come back to find it hopelessly stuck in rain-soaked earth. He and McBride trudged the narrow lane in Wellies covered over with Tyvek slip-ons. There were rows of county and state cars parked against the trees, along with fire and rescue vehicles and a few unmarkeds. A chopper could be heard beating the air somewhere above them.

Sheriff Struthers walked down to meet them, eyes weary and a phone in his vinyl-gloved hand.

"Looks like a total clusterfuck, Sheriff," McBride offered.

"It'll do till one gets here," Elmo said with a bitter smile.

The CID men fell into step with him as they walked up to the clearing ahead.

"What's the overview, Sheriff?" Soames asked.

"There's no short version of this one. I don't think there ever will be."

"A fucking mystery, I hate fucking mysteries," McBride said.

"My partner thinks the answers should be printed in the back of the exam book," Soames said, not unkindly.

The three men stepped between a county van and a firetruck as an ambulance, lights spinning, trundled slowly down the chute toward them. It passed them and picked up speed once it was clear of the gauntlet, the siren growing louder.

"That's some of the kids. Boys." There was something in the sheriff's voice beyond regret, long past remorse.

"How many?" Soames asked.

"Four. They're broken but they're alive. The worst thing, and there's a lot of bad things up here, is the graves in the cellar."

"Graves?" McBride this time.

"We're still countin' 'em." Elmo Struthers stopped then, overcome with emotion. He removed his cap and covered his eyes with a trembling hand.

The two state men stood silent, giving the man all the time he needed. McBride looked ahead to see ribbons of yellow tape strung through the trees. He couldn't recall ever seeing so much police tape.

49

"What kind of trouble are you in?" Jessie Hamer said as she washed her hands in her laundry room sink.

"How much trouble you got?" Levon said. He leaned in the doorway, his back to the kitchen. Teddy Lee sat at the counter, his left arm in a bandage and sling under a fresh work shirt thrown over his shoulders. The suture kit was still open on the countertop. He was sipping a cup of coffee spiked from the bottle of Maker's Mark by his elbow next to a silver pad of tablets. He turned to blink lazily at the dawn light coming in through the window above the sink.

"Tell your cousin to take it easy on those painkillers," she said, drying her hands. "Those are pet meds, and I can't be real sure of the effect they'll have."

"Dog or cat?" Teddy said, voice slurred and juicy.

"Take 'em whole for a dog, break 'em in quarters for a cat," Jessie said, stepping into the kitchen.

"I'm gonna run Teddy over to the bus terminal," Levon said. "Then, I'm outta your hair."

"You coming back later? I got tilapia in the freezer for tonight and Sandy's going to the movies."

"I meant out of your hair for good, Jessie."

She canted her head, eyes slits.

"What the hell, Levon? As in out of my life?"

"I'm not doing you any favors keeping on with whatever this is between us."

"I like whatever this is between us. I like *you*, stupid."

"What have you had since you met me? Hell, you had a pair of murderers come to your house. You and your daughter have been chased through the woods. Now, I'm bringing wanted fugitives to your house to be stitched up. On top of all that, you keeping secrets for me could get you in serious trouble someday."

"It has not been boring, I'll give you that."

"It'd just be better if I stayed shy of you, is all."

"Better for who?"

"For you."

"Not better for you?"

"No."

"Say it," she said, brows knitting.

"Say what?" he said.

"Say why it wouldn't be better for you."

Levon leaned back on the counter and was conscious of how tired he was. He was dirty and bloody and smelled of sweat and sulfur. He'd tracked mud across her kitchen floor. He looked down at his hands, the skin cracked over old calluses.

"Because I'd miss seeing you. I'd miss being with you," he said.

"Get your cousin to the bus and go home and get some sleep," she said. "Dinner's at seven and don't be late or the fried potatoes will get soggy."

There were three buses due to depart the Trailways behind the Waffle House near the interstate. One for Miami, one for Houston, and one for Indianapolis with a change in Memphis.

Levon walked to where Teddy sat hunched on a bench where folks were setting down luggage for a porter to load into the belly of one of the three buses. Teddy was cleaned up in clothes left behind by Jessie's late husband. He wore the sling under a suede coat. Levon had shaved off his cousin's beard and it changed the shape of the man's face. A pair of tinted shades and a handful of hair gel completed the transformation.

Teddy looked with bleary eyes at the ticket envelope Levon placed in his hands. He plucked the ticket out and struggled to focus on it.

"Indiana?" he said, blinking up at Levon.

"You'll get yourself in less trouble there."

"It's boring."

"That's good. You need boring. Boring is good for you." Levon took a seat next to him. He handed over a second packet; a folded-over manila envelope heavy with cash.

Teddy turned to him, raw eyes glistening.

"Why you doin' this for me, Levon?"

"Not sure myself," Levon said. "But I meant what I said before."

Teddy searched his cousin's face.

"You need to never come back here again, Teddy. Go somewhere else and start over. Try doing it right this time."

"How?" Teddy said in a strangled whisper. "How'm I supposed to forget what I done?"

"You're not supposed to forget. You'll never forget. You'll learn to live with it, or you won't. I'm way past caring about that."

"You shoulda left me there. Left me there with Trevor."

"Don't come back here." Levon stood and walked away past the line boarding the bus for the west.

The following day a news item appeared on the front page of the *Atlanta Journal* and in the back sections of other papers when it was included at all.

State Rep Dead in Single Car Crash

(AP) ATLANTA. Representative Aaron Bissonette of Powder Springs, GA, suffered fatal injuries in a single-car accident when his state-assigned vehicle ran off the road on Highway 20 near Greensboro early Friday morning. The cause of the accident is under investigation, but early indications point to hazardous road conditions following heavy rain. Also lost in the crash was State Public Safety Officer Sergeant John Morris Coolidge, a ten-year veteran assigned to Bissonette as a driver. A long career in the state house was distinguished by...

TAKE A LOOK AT: LEVON'S HUNT (LEVON CADE 9)

BY CHUCK DIXON

A DARK AND TWISTED VIGILANTE JUSTICE SERIES THAT IS IMPOSSIBLE TO PUT DOWN.

Levon Cade uncovers more of the conspiracy that cost him the life of a beloved family member. All he wants is to be left alone to raise his daughters, but he can't walk away from finding the men responsible for the death of his young cousin.

His journey into the dark world of child trafficking takes him into a twisted world lying just out of sight. One thing is certain —Levon's hunt will end in blood.

"Dixon's backwoods Southern-fried noir is as compelling as anything by Jim Thompson or Ross MacDonald." – **Mike Baron, author of the Biker Series.**

AVAILABLE NOW

ABOUT THE AUTHOR

Born and raised in Philadelphia, Chuck Dixon worked a variety of jobs from driving an ice cream truck to working graveyard at a 7-11 before trying his hand as a writer. After a brief sojourn in children's books he turned to his childhood love of comic books. In his thirty years as a writer for Marvel, DC Comics and other publishers, Chuck built a reputation as a prolific and versatile freelancer working on a wide variety titles and genres from Conan the Barbarian to SpongeBob SquarePants. His graphic novel adaptation of J.R.R. Tolkien's *The Hobbit* continues to be an international bestseller translated into fifty languages. He is the co-creator (with Graham Nolan) of the Batman villain Bane, the first enduring member added to the Dark Knight's rogue's gallery in forty years. He was also one of the seminal writers responsible for the continuing popularity of Marvel Comics' The Punisher.

After making his name in comics, Chuck moved to prose in 2011 and has since written over twenty novels, mostly in the action-thriller genre with a few side-trips to horror, hardboiled noir and western. The transition from the comics form to prose has been a life-altering event for him. As Chuck says, *"writing a comic is like getting on a roller coaster while writing a novel is more like a long car trip with a bunch of people you'll learn to hate."* His

Levon Cade novels are currently in production as a television series from Sylvester Stallone's Balboa Productions. He currently lives in central Florida and, no, he does not miss the snow.

www.ingramcontent.com/pod-product-compliance
Lightning Source LLC
Chambersburg PA
CBHW010827250626
47169CB00010B/2988